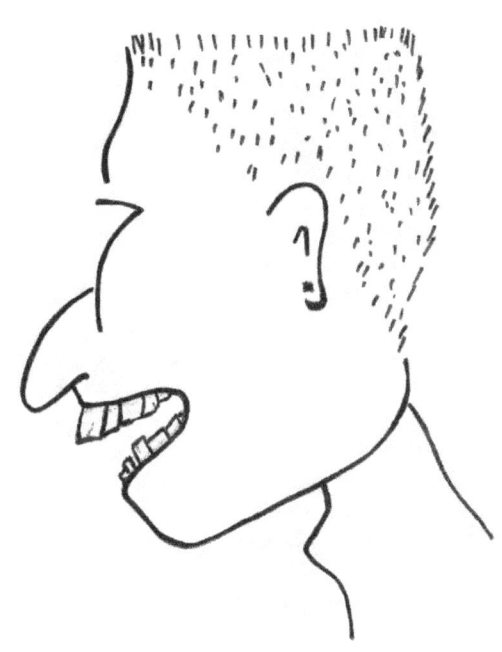

Jughead

By CJ Frye

GRACE
GARLAND
PUBLISHING

Jughead
First Edition
Copyright © 2014 Robert Tyson
ISBN 978-1-941347-02-7

Grace Garland Publishing
P.O. Box 68
Winston, GA 30187
www.GraceGarlandPublishing.com

Ordering Information:
Quantity sales. Special discounts are available on quantity purchases by
corporations, associations, and others. For details, contact the publisher at
the address above.

PUBLISHER'S NOTE:
This book is a work of fiction. Names, characters, places, and incidents
either are the product of the author's imagination or are used fictitiously,
and any resemblance to actual persons, living or dead, business
establishments, events, or locales is entirely coincidental.

Printed in the United States of America.

To my friends…
You know who you are

Table of Contents

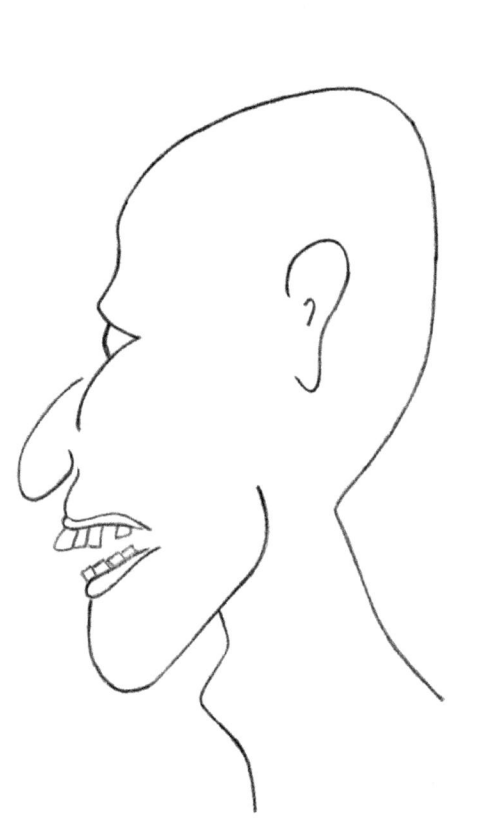

Acknowledgements

The group of people to whom I owe the most thanks is also the group that most likely prefers to remain anonymous. They are all the families of 'Littles' depicted in this book. Over the years, I met these families most everywhere I have traveled. Across the Pacific, over the Atlantic, south of the equator – or right next door – families of Littles thrive everywhere.

I thank all those families for taking me in as one of their own. I also thank God that I never did anything that really pissed any of them off.

For helping me complete my story, I thank Grace Garland Publishing – especially Lynn. Her expertise and enthusiasm is what made this story a reality. I cannot say enough about this company and the personal service they provide.

For editing, I thank Stephanie and Kenny. Their input and attention to detail really brought the story to life.

Finally, I thank you, the reader. I hope you enjoy *Jughead*.

Introduction

As a kid, I grew up next door to a very wild family. My mother forbade me from playing with them but, as a single mother, she worked every day until at least six in the evening. That provided me many opportunities to sneak next door.

My mother discovered my secret trips several times and I faced the consequences, which usually meant I was not able to sit down for a couple of days. For some time afterwards, I would not go next door. However, the draw of the their wild ways always proved too much for me, and I would have to return.

One day my mother came home from work and found welts on me. I tried to hide them but the big red mark on my neck gave me away. There wasn't a shirt collar around that could conceal it. That afternoon, I had played a game with the neighbors called "Wads".

"Wads" was a unique and particularly violent game that the neighbors enjoyed. They would remove the shot pellets from shotgun shells, leaving the plastic 'wad' inside. They then divided into teams and played a game similar to paintball – except with shotguns. The wads were highly inaccurate so you would have to be close to someone in order to hit them. If one of the wads actually struck you, it would leave a nasty mark like the welts my mother was horrified to discover.

Each visit next door promised something equally interesting and dangerous. If I went too long between visits, I missed the heart pounding excitement of their reckless behavior – at least it seemed reckless compared to the rest of my life. It was normal for their lives.

Over the years, I met many people like my childhood neighbors. They exist across all cultures. They stretch the rubber band of acceptability beyond its limits so that it never goes back to its original shape. Sometimes their mere presence is unnerving. They are so untamed compared to the normal order of society that you never know what they will do next – but you know you had better not cross them.

This book is based on experiences with families of Littles, experiences that are sometimes irrational, sometimes senseless, but somehow essential in their lives.

Jughead is just one of those stories.

Chapter 1

———————

Having never shopped at the Piggly Wiggly, I wasn't sure what to expect. I was more used to shopping in the big supermarkets in Atlanta. This small store seemed confining and lacked a wide selection of choices.

I saw the same feelings cross over my wife's face as she scanned the hand-made signs on the windows. One sign advertised a special on pigs feet and beside it was an unbelievable price on ribs.

"It looks clean." Susan, my wife, said optimistically.

"Yes, and we'll save a lot of time by not having to choose between so many different brands." I said, grasping for her optimist straws. I gave her a weak smile.

"Let's go get some pigs feet." Susan smiled as she teasingly punched me on the shoulder.

Our lives had changed drastically. Until then, I had worked in downtown Atlanta for a financial services company. I worked there for almost twelve years, ever since I graduated from college. We lived well in a downtown apartment with fabulous views of the city and a gourmet kitchen. This magnificent kitchen, however, was just for show because we ate out almost every meal.

I was an investment broker and I brought investors into the company hand over fist. I was reaping in fast commissions and spending it almost as fast – sometimes faster. The company compensated me well for my work. I made them millions of dollars and they enabled us to lead a carefree, over-indulgent lifestyle.

Then reality hit. The company went belly-up.

Overstated dividends. Non-existent returns. Fictitious investments.

I found myself as a peddler in a Ponzi scheme. I should have known what was happening. I saw the signs but ignored them. I turned my head at the occasional red flag and never really thought about the people impacted by our frauds – until the trials.

Looking back, I would have done things differently. I certainly would have avoided the traps that eventually convicted my employer.

I was lucky, though. I was not one of the true insiders of the company. I just worked a job like everyone else. My commissions made me a legal target for a while, but a good lawyer and playing stupid, my specialty, kept me out of jail.

In addition, I had invested all my own savings and retirement in the company plans. The same plans that now left thousands of families destitute also left me destitute – or rather 'us'. There is no better way to play stupid than to invest in the same financial schemes that you recommend to others.

When you complain about Sarbanes-Oxley mandates, regulations, and stringency, I'm one of the people to blame. Some of those regulations try to save you from me; others try to save me from myself.

When it was all over, we lost everything material. House, cars, savings, retirement, bank accounts – gone, gone, gone. On the other hand, I was not in jail. That was the one glint of a silver lining that we clung to during those days.

I ended up on long-term probation. I couldn't work in the financial services industry ever again. Since my name was in the newspapers and on TV, most companies would have nothing to do with me. I even became suspicious of companies that showed any interest – they would have to be up to no good if they considered me!

The only reason we had any money at all was my hobby. I had always been good with my hands and I enjoyed working on cars. I restored a 1977 Chevrolet Corvette. I paid cash when I bought it, and when it all came crashing down around us, I sold it for cash. Keeping the money out of the bank accounts kept it away from the IRS, lawyers, and court orders. We had about $3000 left which now seemed like a fortune. That was our nest egg.

After the bank repossessed our house, we weren't able to afford anything near Atlanta so we rented a small house in the woods of South Fulton County, Georgia. I made a deal with the owner to fix the place up to serve for a portion of the rent. I supplied the labor and he furnished the materials.

Now, here we were. Susan and I. Outside the Piggly Wiggly in Palmetto, Georgia – debating pigs feet versus ribs.

"I say we treat ourselves to ribs tonight. Our first night in our new house deserves something special." Susan believed in optimistic attitudes. It just wasn't always possible. We went through depressions and denial and we certainly had our share of arguments but, overall, I would have lost my sanity without her.

"I agree. Let's go see the Pig!"

Chapter 2

_____

"I'll take your groceries out to the car for you. By the way, my name is 'Ronny'." The bagboy at Piggly Wiggly loaded up our cart skillfully. We had a full load, including a pack of ribs on the very top. It was a surprise that the store still carted the food to our car.

"Thank you, Ronny. My car is just across the aisle. I can take it from here." I wasn't used to this sort of service.

"No problem and no tipping. It's the way the manager likes it. Looks like you're setting up house in the area…"

The grinding of tires sliding across gravel and asphalt stopped his words in mid-sentence.

"Hey! Watch where you're going!" A beat-up 80's style Ford pickup ground to a stop with dust and smoke swirling around it, enveloping us. The truck sputtered and the driver raced the engine to keep it running. He stuck his hand out the window, palm up, in a questioning and aggressive manner.

His passenger banged his hand against the side of the truck door and yelled at us, "You trying to get killed?"

Susan and I, frozen in mid-step, quickly stepped back onto the curb beside the bagboy.

"You oughta be more careful, city folk." The driver stared as he eased his truck by us. He spat tobacco juice just a few inches from my foot. Some of the saliva ran down his chin and into his grey beard where it joined the stains from years of chewing.

I felt the hairs on the back of my neck stand up. I didn't like the man's attitude or the whole chain of events. I also didn't like the odds.

There were four people in the front seat of the truck. The driver and the passenger on the other side who had already spoken. I then noticed that the passenger only had one eye. He had an eye patch on the other. He continued to wave his arms in the air at me.

Between the two, sitting next to the driver, was an older woman who I assumed to be the driver's wife. Beside her was a quite striking girl in her early twenties. Her make-up and coiffed hair was a strong contrast to the looks of the others in the truck; however, she was ranting and yelling the loudest. Only the old woman stayed quiet as if she were on a completely different ride from the rest.

In the back of the truck bed were two more people sitting in lawn chairs. One was a boy, about ten years old, wearing a football helmet. It was an old school white helmet with the tinted shield covering his eyes.

The other was a tall, thin man. He had a large head and a very short buzz cut to his blond hair. It almost made him look bald. He had big bucked teeth, big ears, and the largest Adam's apple I had ever seen on a person. His long, lanky arms hung off the arms of the lawn chair.

He glared down at me as they drove by.

"That was scary." Susan's eyes were big.

"Don't say anything yet. You don't want to rile them up." Ronnie held out his hand in caution and stayed on the curb. We took his advice and stood there with him

"Whew!" When the truck finally turned the corner, the bagboy let out a sigh of relief.

"That's the Littles. You don't want to mess with the Littles. In fact, I need to unload your groceries and get back in the store as soon as possible. We have to keep a close eye on them when they shop." The bagboy hurriedly crossed over to the parking lot. "That must be your car over there. I don't recognize it as one of the locals."

"We just moved here. We live out in the Rico area." I finally got my voice back.

Ronnie stopped briefly from loading the packages. "Then you'll probably be seeing a lot of the Littles. They live out in Rico, too. My advice is to stay as far away from them as possible. They're a pretty wild bunch."

"What about the local police? Don't they do anything?" Susan had a concerned look on her face. The look reflected my own thoughts.

"Chattahoochee Valley has jurisdiction out there. They spend their fair share of time at the Littles but with so many of them, there's always some kind of trouble." Ronny finished loading the groceries.

"It was nice meeting you folks." Ronnie held out his hand.

"I'm sorry I didn't introduce us sooner. I'm Roger Multry and this is my wife, Susan." I shook Ronny's hand. He was a wealth of information.

Once we were inside our own truck, with the windows rolled up, the air conditioner on, and the doors locked, we both eased out a sigh of relief.

"We're not in Atlanta anymore." Susan managed a nervous, relieved laugh.

"You're right about that! I thought the girl inside the truck was the scariest. She had wild eyes! Then I saw that tall lanky guy in the back – in a lawn chair! He looked like he was going to jump out on top of me!" I backed out of the parking spot, still keeping a watchful eye out for the Little's truck.

"I hope we don't run into them again anytime soon." Susan rummaged through the grocery bag between us on the seat. She found a pack of cheap chocolate chip cookies, took a couple out, and handed one to me.

"Well. Rico is a small place. Odds are that we'll see the Littles more than we care. We'll have to learn to deal with them and get along." I was trying to exude confidence but there was something innately wild and untamed about the Littles. They lived by their own rules. "We'll have to learn to fit in."

"If we want to fit in, we need to change the way we dress. You have on a button down shirt and khakis and I'm wearing a Hawaiian print shirt. We were probably scarier and more alien to them than they were to us." Susan fanned her hand across the front of her shirt in a mock fashion display. It was her favorite shirt but it was out of place here.

"I didn't get the sense that they were remotely afraid of us. We did get some looks though!" We traveled in silence for a while. The twelve-mile trip back to our house was still unfamiliar and seemed to take a long time.

Chapter 3

We turned into our new driveway, directly off Highway 70. Even though it was a major road, there was little traffic other than the early morning and late afternoon commuters. Beyond that, there was just an occasional local vehicle or tractor.

"I'll put up the groceries if you'll get the grill going. I'm starving!" Susan quickly whisked a double load of grocery bags into the house. I stopped and took a good look at her as she walked off. Her blond hair was wavy and shining. She was a perfect size and kept herself fit throughout the depressing court trials. Most of all, she made her blue jeans look good.

I whistled a wolf call at her and she exaggerated the swing of her hips in response.

"You better get the grill started if you want to see any more!" With a swing of her hair and a quick bat of her eyelashes, Susan disappeared into the house.

Dragging the grill out from under the eaves, I thought it looked sturdy enough. I loaded it with charcoal, squirted on some starter fluid, and while the coals were heating up, I surveyed my new surroundings.

There wasn't much to see. Across the road in front of the house, in the back, and on the left side was all just timberland. The pasture to the right of us contained a herd of cows.

Our driveway circled around in front of the house and pine trees lined it on both sides. The property owner cut the grass but it hadn't been trimmed or groomed. Just a rough cut so we could see any snakes, he said. The owner left the push mower and an old weed eater. Clean up was now my job.

There was not another house in sight. If we went east on Hwy 70 it was at least two miles before you came to another home. There were a couple of dirt roads off the main one so we knew that people must live back in the woods somewhere. We had not been exploring down those roads.

If you went west on Hwy 70 about a quarter of a mile, there was a house across the street with a lot of cars in the yard. Another quarter of a mile from there was an old shack. It was difficult to ascertain if anyone lived in the shack. Susan thought the yard was too clean to be vacant but I never saw anyone there.

Our house needed painting. It peeled in most places, and other spots badly needed repair. The steps were a hazard at best. Although enclosed at one time, the back porch now had screen wire hanging from it in shambles.

Everywhere I looked, something needed repairing.

"Are you ready for the ribs?" Susan called out of the kitchen window. The old house didn't have air-conditioning so all the windows were open on this hot August day.

"Ready." I opened the grill lid and watched the coals burning red and white. The ribs sizzled as I put them on the hot grate. They were nice ribs – and cheap – my new favorite.

I found an old picnic table bench, dusted it off, and pulled it over for us to have a place to sit.

"I know that you're worried but it will be okay. Last week we didn't know where we would live and now just look around. You found us a cheap place to stay and a deal on a truck with an air conditioner! Now we're about to eat ribs in our fabulous outside dining area." Susan motioned around the general area. Like I said, she is always the optimist.

"But…" I stopped mid-sentence. The coals in the bottom of the grill made a shifting sound, the entire bottom of the grill crashed to the ground and the coals scattered on impact. I opened the lid and the ribs were still sitting there on the grate but the coals were on the ground.

We looked at each other and started to laugh.

"I'll heat up the oven to cook the ribs." Susan went back into the house, still laughing.

Chapter 4

I looked around for a shovel to clean up the coals but before I could find one, I heard the sound of a pickup turning into our driveway.

Slowly pulling off the highway was the old tan and brown truck from the Piggly Wiggly. The Littles were coming for a visit.

"Howdy neighbor!" The old man driving the truck waved out the window at me. The whole family wasn't with him this time. Beside him in the front seat were the young girl and the one-eyed man. The tall, lanky man was still sitting in the back of the truck in his lawn chair.

"Sorry that we got off on the wrong foot back in town. I didn't know we were going to be neighbors. Ma said that I should come by and make amends. You never know when you might need a friend." The old man climbed slowly out of the truck.

"I'm William Little; folks around here just call me 'Pa' or 'Grandpa' depending on your age." Mr. Little extended his hand and we shook. He had a surprisingly strong handshake and he reinforced it with a little extra squeeze before he released my hand.

"Good to meet you, Mr. Little. My name is Roger Multry. My wife, Susan, is inside." I was apprehensive but felt it was best to be friendly.

"Call me 'Pa'! This here fellow getting out of the truck is Steve Johnson Little. We call him 'Patch'. He lost his eye trying to pull a nail out of a tree. The string was wrapped around the nail and Patch thought he would just pull on the string and pull out the nail. Well, wouldn't you know it, he pulled hard and that nail came out, flew straight back and stuck in his eye. Awful mess. Ma says it was our fault for naming him after 'Patch' on the soap operas. She said it predestined him or some such nonsense.

"That pretty little girl in front of the truck there is Tammy Randall Little, you know, from the soap The Doctors.

"What can I say? The wife likes to name kids after soap opera people. We have a Marlena, and a Luke, and a Victor and a Vic. From both Another World and General Hospital.

"You might know Tammy better as 'Lil' Tami'. She's quite famous out at Fannie's on Fulton Industrial. A big draw, especially when she does her Ping-Pong ball trick.

"In back of the truck there is Stanley Little. When he was born, Ma said he was special and not suited for a soap opera name. She said he sure looked like a Stanley though!" Pa Little nodded towards the tall man in back with the extraordinarily long arms.

"Most people don't call him 'Stanley'. Most call him 'Jughead'." Patch walked up to us laughing. Crusty material oozed from beneath his eye patch.

Mr. Little turned on Patch in an instant and grabbed him by the shirt. "I told you not to call him that."

I understood how the name, Jughead, fit the man in the back of the truck. His head was an abnormal size. The closely cropped hair and blond eyebrows made him look hairless. His large Adam's apple was still astonishing to me as was every sharp feature and awkward angle of his posture.

Jughead – Stanley, rather – hopped out of the back of the truck. He was more than a full head taller than me. He probably topped six feet ten inches. He held out a big hand full of knuckles towards me in the form of a handshake.

"My friends call me 'Jughead'. It's from the bubble gum cartoons. You better call me 'Stanley'." When Jughead spoke, the smell of his breath rocked me back on my heels. His teeth were yellow, cracked, and caked in food remnants. His voice had a flat sound like he was talking with a mouth full of cotton, accentuated by the severely bucked teeth.

When I shook his hand, I thought he would crush my fingers in his grip. "I got the strongest grip of anybody. Isn't that right, Pa?"

"You bet it is, Stanley! Nobody has a grip like yours. Now you'd better let that city fellow's hand go or he might not be able to write tomorrow." Mr. Little gently separated Jughead's hand from mine.

"What can I do for you, Mr. Little?" I discretely rubbed my sore fingers.

"I just wanted to come by and welcome you folks to the neighborhood. We might have gotten off on the wrong foot, what with you stepping off that curb in front of us but we're your closet neighbors so we'll just let bygones be bygones.

"We live just down the road there on the left. We have a couple of cars for sale out front. You can't miss it. Anytime you need anything, just feel free to call on us." Mr. Little spat a stream of tobacco towards the base of one of the trees.

"Yeah. We wouldn't want you to think we were unfriendly or anything. We can be the friendliest people around." Lil' Tami leaned out of the driver's side window sucking lovingly on a Tootsie Roll Pop. "Pa, give him one of my cards. Me and my girlfriends are available for private parties. We give discounts to family and good looking neighbors."

"Here's one of her cards. Lil' Tami's Playhouse, escort service, and exotic dancing." Mr. Little reached into his overall bib pocket and handed me a quite explicit business card describing Lil' Tami's business. "She's at Fannie's almost every night – except Monday. She has the parole officer on Mondays."

"Yeah. Me, too." Those words inadvertently spilled out of my mouth before I knew it.

"Oh. You have to see the parole officer, too. Maybe we can ride together." Lil' Tami leaned further out the window, almost releasing her cleavage from its confines.

"Get back in the truck Tami. He's got his own woman. Good looking thing, too. I bet she really takes care of you." Patch waved Lil' Tami back inside the truck. "She just can't stop advertising."

"Well, we're going to head back towards the house. Good meeting you, Roger. We'll be seeing a lot more of you. Looks like you got a little problem with your grill there." Mr. Little pointed towards my smoldering coals on the ground as his clan climbed back to their various positions. He cranked up his huffing, smoking beast of a truck.

"No, we just like really rare meat." I replied straight-faced.

Pa Little looked at me quizzically, as if trying to determine if I was kidding.

About that time, the ten-year-old boy with the football helmet came peddling a unicycle down the road. He held a bicycle bell in his hand and rang the bell every few feet.

"That's Yuri Little. You know, from Days of Our Lives." Mr. Little backed out of the drive without looking either way.

He stopped his truck with a lurch, stuck his head out the window, and yelled at the boy, "Don't be late for dinner, Yuri!" With that, he sped off down the road.

Chapter 5

"What was that all about? I saw you had visitors and decided to stay inside in case I needed to dial 911." Susan was only half kidding. The phone was still in her hand.

"It's okay. Just a portion of the Little clan coming by to welcome us to Rico. I met Patch, Lil' Tami, Yuri, and Stanley. On yeah, Mr. Little wants us to call him 'Pa'. And Lil' Tami will give us a discount on all our party needs." I handed Susan Lil' Tami's business card.

"Oh! An escort service. She's quite an entrepreneur. What did Pa Little have to say about it?" Susan flicked the card onto the counter.

"He's the one who gave me the card. I think he's her manager or something like that. Wow! It smells wonderful in here!" I walked around the kitchen, surprised at its transformation.

"Don't wander far. Dinner will be ready soon." Susan went back to work on the meal.

"It looks great! You really did a good job." I was astonished at what she accomplished in the kitchen. She put the pots, pans, and dishes into the cabinets. The china cabinet was already organized and the table was set. Gone were the empty boxes and the four full ones that remained were neatly stacked in the corner.

"Well. It's home. By the way, Maintenance Man, we need some more outlets." Susan waved towards the one outlet in the room.

By the time we ate dinner and washed the dishes, it was already getting dark.

"Are you ready for your first day in your new job tomorrow?" Susan sat down on the front step, enjoying the cooler evening air.

"I found my tools and have them ready. Found my mechanic's coveralls, too. Just remember, I might not be paid and even then, I might not be paid much. He's only giving me a job as a favor to Charlie." I didn't want her to get too excited.

Charlie and I were members of the same car club, Marietta Street Rods. We usually hung out together at the club events. One of the things I liked about the club was that it didn't matter who you were, where you were from, or where you worked. We were all there because we liked cars.

Charlie hooked me up with the job at Buddy's Auto Service. Buddy, the owner and the namesake, made it clear that I only received pay for work on car repairs, not for sales of gas and oil. No salary. My payment comes from the billable time I work on cars – and Buddy gets the bulk of that.

"Besides, I'm not a trained mechanic. I worked on our hobby cars but I might not know enough to make it as a mechanic – or mechanic's helper. Buddy said what he needed was a 'monkey who can turn a wrench'." I was going from an Investment Broker in the heart of downtown Atlanta, with office views that spanned the city landscape, to a job as a wrench monkey with a questionable paycheck. Nothing wrong with the job, but it sure was a big change.

"I hope you interviewed better than that! I know you and love you but I wouldn't hire you with that sort of negative attitude. Be positive. You have a job opportunity. It might work out, it might not, but you have the chance. It's more than we've had for a while and we can certainly use any money that comes our way." Susan was right. I had been jobless ever since the firm failed.

"I'll try to be more positive, but you have to admit this is a big career change for me. I had over a thousand connections on LinkedIn but not a single person came forward to offer any help. No one. The only person who helped us was Charlie from the car club. So much for Social Networking." I snorted in disgust.

"Let's turn in so you can get a good night's sleep. It's a new day tomorrow. New home. New job. New career. I'm so excited, I can't wait for tomorrow to be here!" Susan jumped up and almost skipped into the house.

"What an optimist." I muttered under my breath.

The sound of a bicycle bell made me turn and look back towards the road. Riding down the middle of the road was Yuri, on his unicycle with his white football helmet, ringing the bicycle bell every few feet.

"Hi Yuri!" I waved to my new neighbor.

By the dim evening light, it was difficult to tell, but I think he gave me the finger.

I went inside the house, closed the door, and secured the lock.

Chapter 6

"What the hell is all that noise?" I sat straight up in the bed and looked over at the clock. "It's 2:15 in the morning!"

Susan groaned, rolled over, and covered her head with a pillow.

The noise from a booming stereo pierced the previous quiet of the night. With no air conditioning, the tune of 'Sweet Home Alabama' floated through our open bedroom window. The song was intermixed with raucous laughter, a thumping bass, and the intermittent sound of roaring mufflers.

Scrambling out of bed, I made my way to the front yard. Down the road, the Littles were fully awake. Bright lights from their house cast an eerie glow up into the trees. A car pulled into their driveway and blew its horn to announce their arrival.

It was definitely a party.

Outside the house, individual voices were clearer but the words ran together – just a dull roar of sound penetrating the night air. Occasionally, one or two voices would stand out as over-exuberant partygoers whooped their happiness to the world.

I sat down on the front steps as another car departed and sounded its horn.

As it pulled out of the driveway, this car turned eastward onto the road past our house, and blew the horn in two long intervals. I assumed they were saying goodbye. After watching several cars come and go, I thought I saw a pattern to the greetings. The arriving cars gave two short, almost happy honks as a form of 'Hello.' Departing cars gave two longer honks once on the highway as a 'Goodbye'. Cars that were just driving by would sound two short beeps of the horn, which I assumed was like a wave.

"If your car horn doesn't work you're completely out of the social circle." Susan spoke from the doorway. Startled, I nearly fell off the steps.

"Don't sneak up on me like that! I almost had a heart attack!" I was trying to recompose myself.

"What's going on?" Susan just laughed at me.

"I think it's a party. It's the most traffic I've seen on the road since we've been here. The Littles must be night owls." I stood up to go back inside.

"Think you should go talk to them? You need to get some sleep." Susan looked down the road towards the Little's house.

"It's just one party. They'll probably get tired soon and go to bed. Better to just let it be. Besides, being new to the neighborhood, we don't want to get on Mr. Little's bad side. Let them have their party and we'll just do our best to sleep through it." It was much too early in our new home to start criticizing the neighbors. "Let's go back to bed."

I spent the rest of the night listening to the Little's party. Every time I almost fell asleep, there would be an unusually loud noise, or a car would come or go and sound its horn.

My alarm clock finally went off at 6:30am and the party was just winding down. There were a few remaining beeps of horns as cars left the Little's house. With only a small amount of sleep, it was time for me to shower and get ready for my first day at work.

Buddy's Auto Service was located over in Palmetto, about twelve miles from where we now lived. Buddy did a reasonable business in gas sales and oil changes, but he was most widely known for his knowledge and skills with older vehicles.

Buddy's shop was already open so I went into the grungy office to introduce myself. The years as an auto repair office created a thin film of garage patina on everything in the office. The unmistakable smells of solvent and penetrating oil, along with a faint whiff of carbon monoxide exhaust, hung in the air.

Sitting at a massive desk, a man was busy working on a four-barrel carburetor. His reading glasses rode low on his nose. Parts of a rebuild kit were strewn across the desktop. He was a slender man with remarkably well-groomed hair. He wore brown shop clothes with the name 'Buddy' over the left pocket. He was intent on his task and did not hear me enter the room.

"Excuse me. Buddy? My name is Roger Multry. We talked on the phone last week." I held out my hand for a handshake.

"Hi, Roger. I didn't hear you come in." He returned my greeting with a firm but greasy handshake. "You're early. That's good. Charlie vouched for you. Said you're good with a wrench. We'll see about that. I've had a lot of people come and go who thought they were good wrench monkeys.

"First, let's be clear about the work. I can't afford to pay you a salary. You get paid for the time that you work on clients' vehicles – period. If there's no work, there's no pay – but you still have to be here. No telling when a car will come in.

"I expect you to help out around the shop. Most everybody pays for their gas with a card at the pump. Sometimes though, we actually get cash. I'm hoping you know how to make change, right?"

Buddy was reeling off the rules so quickly that I almost missed the question. "Yes. Right. Sure I can make change."

"Good. Charlie said you were 'college educated'. When you work on a car, I'll tell you what to do. All you do is take off the parts I tell you to take off, clean the parts I tell you to clean, and re-install the parts when I tell you. Got it?" Buddy was only a few years older than me but he was definitely in charge.

"No problem. Like we discussed on the phone, I'll do whatever you tell me to do. I just want to make you happy with my work. I really need this job to work out." I was completely honest with Buddy about my situation. Charlie is the only reason he decided to try me.

"Just don't make me mad and we'll do alright. Come on. I'll show you around." Buddy walked around the garage and showed me where everything was located. There wasn't a lot to show – an office, a storage room in back, and four garage bays.

"Most of those cars over there belong to me. Just waiting to get them fixed up to sell. A couple of cars belong to customers who can't pay for their repairs yet." Buddy pointed to the cars in front of the garage, all neatly lined up along the side of his parking lot.

"Back here though … back here is the gold mine." I followed Buddy down a driveway that ran alongside the building and to the back of his garage. An eight-foot high chain link fence with a privacy screen prevented unwanted eyes from peering inside.

Buddy pulled out his key ring, unlocked the gate, and swung the doors open. In the back of his garage was a wondrous sight. Amid the grass and briars were rows and rows of classic cars. These were not restored cars by any means but they were a treasure trove of parts and chassis in all states of preservation – or decay – depending on your view.

"Wow! This is awesome!" I was truly impressed. So many classic car models had all but disappeared following years of destruction for scrap metal, crushed one by one.

"Yup. One of the best classic car junk yards around." Buddy smiled with pride at his collection. "You need a bumper for a Studebaker? I have it. How about gutter guards for a '68 AMX? I have two. If I don't have it, I'll find it for you."

"I can see why you have such a good fence. People would rob you blind for these parts." I was still in awe at the vintage junk yard.

"That's exactly what happened with the last wrench monkey that worked for me. He was coming back at night to clean me out. I've added a few touches since then." Buddy pointed towards cameras at the corners of the building and on the light poles at each corner of the lot. "All those cameras are tied in centrally and I can monitor them from my phone."

"Impressive. There's cars here I've only seen in books and car shows." It was a car lover's paradise.

"Nobody comes back here without me." Buddy looked at me over the rims of his sunglasses – a look that accentuated his statement.

"No problem, Buddy."

"Okay. Let's get back to work. There are a couple of cars that need an oil change." Buddy clapped his hands and rubbed the palms together.

Buddy gave me an overview of his oil change process with the first car. Then he turned me loose on the second, an aging Chrysler Sebring. He checked my work carefully before grunting his approval.

By lunchtime, I had changed the oil on two more cars. Buddy checked on me several times and grunted his satisfaction at my progress.

"Lunchtime!" Buddy came out of the office holding up his lunch bag. "If you didn't bring lunch you can try the truck stop next door. I'd stick to the burgers and fries though."

Instead, I just grabbed a Coke and a pack of Lance crackers from Buddy's vending machine and had a quick, cheap snack. Afterwards, I cleaned up around the garage, sweeping and throwing away the obvious trash.

"That's all the oil changes today unless someone else comes in. The Olds in bay number two needs the radiator replaced. How about you remove the radiator and let me know when you're done. Think you can handle that?" I thought I'd be doing oil changes all day, but Buddy switched it up on me.

"Sure. I'm on it."

By quitting time, the radiator was out and I took care of a couple more oil changes. I laid out the radiator and parts for Buddy to look over. I thought one of the hoses needed replacing but that was Buddy's call.

"Good job today, Roger. See you in the morning about nine? I'll get the parts for the Olds and you can put it back together." Buddy agreed on the replacement hose.

"I thought I'd come in around eight o'clock. I can have the Olds knocked out fairly early and can get on to the next car." I was a morning person anyway, so I might as well be working.

"Great! I'll see you in the morning." Buddy turned to leave but he stopped, reached into his pocket, and pulled out a pair of mechanics gloves.

"Here. These will help protect your knuckles and make it easier to work on warm engines." He threw the gloves to me.

"Thanks, Buddy. For everything." I reached out for a handshake.

"Don't thank me yet, you still haven't been paid!" Buddy shook my hand and slapped me on the shoulder.

[48]

Chapter 7

"What the hell is all that noise?" I sat straight up in the bed and looked over at the clock. "It's 2:15 in the morning!"

I felt like I was in a scene from the movie Groundhog Day. Susan groaned, rolled over, and covered her head with a pillow.

A party last night was understandable, sort of. A party again tonight was too much!

I got out of bed, went to the front porch, and sat down on the stoop. There was a party at the Littles but it was different from the night before. There were fewer cars going in and out and the music was different, more dance music than Southern Rock.

I watched and listened for a while until Susan finally joined me.

"Another party?" She said in the middle of her yawn.

"Yep, another party."

"Do you think this happens every night?"

"Hope not. If it happens again tomorrow night I'll talk to Mr. Little about it." I didn't relish the idea of the discussion with Pa Little but I also needed my sleep. "Let's go back to bed and try to rest even if we can't sleep."

The next day at work, I was really dragging. I felt I had to talk to Buddy so he would know what was going on. I related the recent events.

"The Littles? Are you any kin to them?" Buddy's reaction left no doubt that this was a deal breaker.

"No. No. We're just neighbors, but for the last two nights they've been up all night partying." I wanted to set the record straight and distance myself from the Littles.

"Well, you better get used to it. After the strip joints close down on Fulton Industrial, the Littles open up Lil' Tami's Playhouse. It's an afterhours party house. They even have an old airport shuttle van. They take whole groups from Fannie's to their house and then take them back the next morning."

"You mean every night?" I asked incredulously.

"Every night except Monday. I think Lil' Tami has the parole officer on Monday so she takes the whole day off." It seemed everyone knew about Lil' Tami's parole officer schedule.

"I had no idea. I'll have to talk to Mr. Little."

"You do that!" Buddy let out a little snort of a laugh. "I don't think Pa Little is going to care about your beauty sleep. My advice to you is to learn to sleep through it. There's always some strange goings-on at their shack. You don't want to get mixed up in it."

"If it happens again tonight, I'll have to talk to him." I nodded my head in bold, although ignorant, confidence.

"Good luck. You heard my advice. I have lived here my whole life. Heard a lot of tales about the Littles. Know a lot of them to be true. Avoid them at all costs. Be cordial if cornered but be on your toes whenever you're around them." Buddy spoke from the voice of experience.

When I arrived home that night, both Susan and I were dragging, tired from the lack of sleep. We turned in early, hoping to get a few hours in before the Littles opened their party doors.

"If they start again tonight, I'm going to talk to them." I told Susan as we were getting the bed ready, hoping she would have a better idea than a confrontation.

"I agree. I'm sure he'll understand. Besides, who has a party every night of the week?" Susan was, as always, the optimist.

"Well, according to Buddy, it's their business. When the strip bars close, their party opens – every night except Monday. If I can go to sleep right now, I can get four hours in before they start up." I jumped into bed, closed my eyes immediately, and pretended to snore.

"Okay, Rip Van Winkle. You might want to see this before you go to sleep." Susan flicked on the television. "Basic cable! They hooked it up today."

"All right! That should put me to sleep." It was very comforting to watch reruns of the King of Queens.

I slept very well until 2:15am when the music cranked up again. I would have to talk to Pa Little. I only called him 'Pa' in my head. I vowed to myself that I would call him 'Mr. Little' to his face. I didn't relish the idea of him being my 'Pa'.

As I put on my clothes, I prepared myself for the upcoming conversation. I would reason with him. Let him know that I had a job and needed my sleep. I needed my rest to be fully functional the next day. Even in my mind, none of those reasons offset a good party.

Still, I had to talk to Pa Little. Maybe it's because of my own feelings of lost control, for having lost everything, for scraping by to maintain a remote resemblance to our former life. Maybe it was to show Susan that I still had some backbone remaining that the legal system had not surgically removed. Whatever the reasons, I had to stand up to them.

"I'm going to have a talk with Mr. Little." I patted Susan on her hip and headed towards the door.

"Maybe you should wait. It's the middle of the night. It might not be the best time to go over there." Susan had a point.

"Well. I'm awake. They're obviously awake. The problem is happening now. It seems like a good time."

"You shouldn't go mad."

"I'm not mad. I just want to discuss it with him. I won't start any trouble. We'll just talk. But, just in case, if you don't hear from me in an hour, call the police." With that, I left.

Pulling into the Little's driveway, I saw several cars about, including the shuttle van Buddy mentioned. Cranked up loud and raunchy, the party music blared. The bass was so strong that I was surprised any glass remained in the windows of the house.

I closed my car door and walked no more than three steps when a man stepped out of the dark.

"Can I help you?" He shined a light directly in my face.

"I'm Roger Multry from next door. I wanted to see Mr. Little." I squinted from the light.

"Oh. Mr. Multry. It's me, Patch." Patch shined the light on his face, a sight that really did not help matters. The strange shadows mixed with the eye patch and crust only seemed to make the situation worse.

"Just go on in. Pa usually hangs around the bar area. No use to knock. They wouldn't hear you anyway. Don't mind the dogs either, if I don't bark, they don't bite!" Patch motioned me towards a door at the end of the building.

A couple of dogs came slinking out of the shadows, sniffing at my ankles and heels. They uttered low growls of caution. I held my own and walked straight to the door.

I thought the music was loud outside, but inside it was deafening. The room was an addition to the original structure and ran the length of the entire house. An assortment of Christmas tree lights crisscrossed the ceiling, flashing and blinking in random patterns.

In the middle of the room was a stripper pole. Lil' Tami was performing her art on the pole to the tune of 'Angel Is a Centerfold'. She wore the shortest pair of cut off, Daisy Duke blue jeans shorts I had ever seen. The only remnants from the original shorts were the waistband and the top of the pockets. She also wore a see through halter-top and a pair of cowboy boots. Her strawberry blond hair flowed wildly as she swung around the pole. She commanded the attention of about eight partygoers who were whooping and hollering, sticking dollar bills in her outfit whenever, and wherever, they got the chance.

There were other similarly dressed girls sitting on the couches and chairs with a few clientele. On the coffee table in front of the couch was a mirror with a few lines of cocaine, or meth. One of the girls leaned over, snorted a line, and then looked over at me and smiled while she cleaned the residue off her nose.

At my end of the room, next to the door, was a small bar. Leaning back against the bar, Pa Little contently watched the proceedings. Next to him, sitting on a bar stool, was Jughead.

Jughead was obviously tense. He sat on the edge of the stool as if he were going to burst into action at any moment. He clenched and unclenched his big, boney hands into fists. The veins on his head stood out, throbbing and pulsating.

"Mr. Multry! Glad to see you here. You know you're welcome anytime but tonight is a private party." Pa Little was in his usual attire, farmer's overalls, no shirt, and a Pabst Blue Ribbon beer.

"Hello, Mr. Little. I really didn't come out for the party. It's just that the noise…" I didn't finish my sentence because Jughead butted in.

"He's making me mad, Pa!" Jughead sprayed the words all over Pa and me. I involuntarily flinched from his rancid breath. Jughead pointed towards the corner of the dance floor. A man was putting a dollar bill in Lil' Tami's shorts but he was getting very intimate with the placement. Tami egged him on by standing closer and stroking his hand and the back of his head. She had the man all worked up and he fed her dollar bills as fast as he peeled them off his bankroll.

"Now, Stanley. You know that's Lil' Tami's job. You can't get mad every time she has fun with someone. She's working. Sit back down and calm yourself. I'll let you know when anybody gets out of hand." Pa motioned Jughead to the stool.

"You were saying, Mr. Multry." Pa turned back to me.

"You can call me 'Roger'. What I want to talk to you about is the noise. I know we're a ways up the road but the music and constant horn blowing is keeping us up at night." There, I said it.

Pa Little looked at me thoughtfully for a moment; spat his tobacco juice into a red Solo cup, and then he spoke in a slow and deliberate voice. "Well, Roger, I didn't tell you to move into that house up the road. This is our business – Lil' Tami's Playhouse. We give people a place to go after the clubs close. Besides, you're the only one complainin'.

"I know you're new around here and don't know our ways so I'll tolerate your ignorance – this time. We mind our own business and we don't like people buttin' in. My suggestion to you is that you go home, get in bed with that sweet little wife of yours, and learn to live with it." Pa Little punctuated the last sentence by pointing at me with his beer can.

"We have to work out something. I have to work. I don't want to be rude, but I do have rights and this is excessive noise." I was digging a hole for myself but to stop talking was beyond me.

"Rights!" Pa Little spat the word out causing a spray of Pabst to escape. "Usually when folks mention rights they're talking about the law. I'll show you your rights. Alexandra, go get your Daddy."

Pa Little beckoned to the scantily clad girl on the couch who had just snorted the cocaine. She immediately jumped up and left the room through a door that connected the Playhouse to the rest of the house.

Within seconds a uniformed Deputy bustled through the door, took a position beside Pa Little, and gave me the eye. He had one hand resting on his Beretta. "What's the trouble here, Pa?"

"I don't think there's going to be any trouble. Me and our new neighbor were just having a discussion about 'rights'." Pa Little made little air quotes around the word 'rights' which would have been humorous under different circumstances. "Roger Multry, this is Deputy Justus Little – you know, from General Hospital. Justus is a deputy for the Chattahoochee Valley police department. They have jurisdiction here. Justus, why don't you explain the way 'rights' work around here. Use words that are easily understood by someone on probation."

Leaning back against the bar, Pa Little took another swig of his Pabst, emptied the contents, and crushed the can in his hand.

"Mr. Multry. We don't take to troublemakers around here. If you're on probation then maybe we should step outside to my car. I can run your name through the system and make sure there aren't any outstanding warrants. It may take a while though. I'm very thorough. May even have to take you down to the office. From the looks of things, I see that you're around some illegal drugs over there. I'm sure that's a probation violation." Talking in a slow Southern drawl, Deputy Justus pulled out his handcuffs as he spoke.

"Naw. I don't think you'll have to do that Justus. I think Roger gets the point." Pa Little pushed himself away from the bar. "Roger, my advice to you is to mind your own business. If you don't like our party sounds, then move or get earplugs. If you want to cause trouble, you might get more trouble than you bargained for, especially with probation hanging over your head."

"I have to get back to my rounds. Give me a call if you have any problems. I know where he lives. I think I'll go ahead and run him through the computer. I like to know who lives around me." With that, Deputy Justus left. Pulling out into the road in his cruiser, he chirped the siren a couple of times, and hit the blue lights for a second. Just another voice in the night.

"So, Roger. Do we understand each other? You're welcome to come by and party with us anytime, just like anyone else – but you don't cause trouble. If you do, you better pray that it's the police that come get you." With that, Pa Little reached into a cooler behind the bar and popped open another Pabst.

Lil' Tami and her amorous client were now sitting in a chair together. With all the drinking and partying, the man's inhibitions were completely gone. He was all over Lil' Tami. His hands were groping feverishly as he tried to remove her clothes. Lil' Tami giggled and fended him off expertly, a true professional.

Jughead was in an agitated state. While Deputy Justus was in the room, Jughead continued his vigilance over Lil' Tami and her guest. He was so physically upset that he hit himself in the head a few times in anger.

Pa Little nodded towards Lil' Tami. "Stanley, he's gone too far. Go take care of your sister."

Pa Little gave Stanley the order he was waiting for.

Leaping off the stool, Jughead crossed the room in a second. Grabbing the man by the back of his shirt, Jughead pulled him out of the chair and slammed him to the floor. The man wasn't a small person but Jughead's onslaught left him no opportunity to defend himself.

"Get him, Jughead! He had his hands all over me!" Lil' Tami encouraging Jughead caught me by surprise. Once all giggles and wiggles with the man on the chair, now that his bankroll was gone her allegiance switched back to Jughead.

Jughead needed no encouragement. He pounded his big, boney knuckles into the man's face, neck, and head. Pulling him up off the floor, Jughead rammed his knee into the man's stomach. Slamming him back down, he planted several kicks into the man's ribs with the toe of his steel-toed work boots.

Seeing their companion in trouble, the man's friends tried to help him. From his pocket, Pa Little pulled out a small air horn used on boats and sounded a single, blaring blast from the horn.

In seconds, the room swarmed with Littles. Large and small, young and old, the Little men streamed into the party room. With them, they brought guns, ball bats, and a couple of machetes. It took the fight right out of the partiers and they backed off and watched as Jughead continued his rampage on their friend.

"That's enough!" Pa Little made his announcement.

Jughead though, was out of control. He continued beating the man who was already unconscious. The beating he took was reminiscent of a bull riding video I had once seen. Knocked out early in his ride, the bull rider was still strapped to the bull, which dragged, stomped, and twisted the rider's limp body all over the arena. In this case, Jughead was the bull.

It took several of the Littles to drag Jughead off. Even then, Jughead was still fighting and clawing, trying to get his hands back on the man.

"He made me mad!" Wild-eyed, Jughead yelled as they hauled him away from the beaten and bleeding patron. "He touched Tami! He shouldn't touch Tami!"

"So, Roger." Pa Little said my name as if he didn't like the sound of it. "You really don't want to make anyone mad, do you?"

"You're right, Mr. Little. I don't want to make anyone mad. I'll take your advice and learn to live with the noise – or party music as you call it." To leave, I would have agreed to anything at that moment. Pa Little made the consequences clear and Jughead gave a convincing demonstration. They made no attempt to disguise the threat.

"Great! We understand each other! Remember, you're welcome to come over anytime and party with us. Next time, bring the missus with you. We'll even let her have a turn on the dance pole! She's a cute little thang." Pa Little slapped me on the back in a neighborly fashion except overly hard and with a not-so-gentle push towards the door.

When I was back in my truck, I heaved a sigh of relief. Pulling into the road, I resisted a momentary desire to beep the horn as I drove off.

"So that's it? That's the solution? We have to live with it?" Susan asked incredulously after I relayed the chain of events to her.

"Compared to what Jughead did to their paying client, it sounded like a very reasonable resolution." We were sitting in the kitchen. The Little's music was still blaring. It was 4:15am.

"When you were gone over an hour, I called the police. They said they were aware of the situation and already had an officer at that location. Then I saw the blue lights flash so I felt better." Susan's hands were shaking a little as she sipped her cup of coffee.

"Well, that would be Deputy Justus – Justus Little – from General Hospital. He was already there when I arrived. He's definitely an enforcer for the rest of the family. Probably already run my name through their database. We now know where we stand with the local police." I held my head in my hands. I was tired.

"Did we make a mistake? Was moving here the wrong thing to do?" Susan was almost in tears.

"We have nowhere else to go. I made the mistake a long time ago. We're just trying to recover and there were no other choices. We'll adjust and make it work." Smiling at her, I reached over and held her hand.

"So, how do you think I would do on the stripper pole?" Susan wiped away her tears and managed to muster up a weak smile.

Chapter 8

————————

"In the middle of the night? You went to the Littles and asked them to turn down their stereo – while they were having one of their special parties? That took big balls and a small brain. I had you pegged for a much smarter person than that! You are lucky – you know that don't you?" Shaking his head, Buddy added a grunt of disgust when I relayed the story to him.

"I didn't know it was a real business. I thought they were just partying, which sounds even stupider now that I said it out loud." Buddy was right, I was lucky. If Pa Little had turned Jughead loose on me, I would have been the recipient of his wrath.

"You know, the Littles won't leave you alone. If you're their enemy, they'll make your life miserable until they get even. If you're their friend, they'll make your life miserable by making you part of their drama. Either way – you're screwed. It's best if the Littles don't even know you exist. I tried to warn you." Pulling down one of the bay doors, Buddy pointed his finger at his own chest. "But I should have told you about Deputy Justus."

"That would have been good information to have." I pulled down the last bay door. We were closing up.

"The good news is that it's Friday and pay day. Your check is over there on the desk. I can cash it for you." We were in his office and Buddy locked the front door.

"Thanks. It's not a good idea for me to have a bank account. When the IRS finds it, they seize the account immediately. Cash works best for me right now." I opened the envelope. "Buddy, this is more than I expected."

"Well. I appreciate your help. Showed up on time, did what you were told, cleaned up between jobs, and you're decent with a wrench. Can't ask for more than that in this business." Buddy waved his hand at me in dismissal. "By the way, there's a few of us getting together tonight. If you're up to it, you and Susan are welcome to join us."

"That really sounds good. I'll check with Susan but I bet she'll be glad to get out of the house. Where and what time?"

"Don't get too excited! The place is a dump but they have cheap, cold beer and the only pool tables around. It's called the Turn On Inn at the Fairburn road exit off I-85. The sign on the roof says that it's the 'Barrett Building' but that was a long time ago. You can't miss it. We meet there around seven but folks come and go all evening. See you there." Buddy climbed into his vintage '50 Ford rat rod, fired up the flathead V8, and was gone.

When I arrived home and told Susan about Buddy's invitation, she bubbled over with excitement at the prospect of going anywhere. Dump or no dump, getting out of the house sounded wonderful to her.

Turn On Inn was easy to find. It was still daylight so we saw the building clearly. Buddy was right – the place was a dump. The parking lot consisted of dirt and gravel. Besides a few cars, the other parked vehicles included some work trucks, motorcycles, and one dual wheeled truck pulling a backhoe.

The building itself was a basic block structure – no frills. Fluorescent lights, most of them functional, lined the front. On a stool outside the nondescript front door sat a hefty fellow wearing a black t-shirt with "Security" in white across the front and back.

"Looks like our kind of place! And the sign out front says 'No guns, No knives, No

Cover Charge'. There's Buddy's car over there." I parked next to the flat black '50 Ford.

"I like the name. I'm not sure if it means to 'turn on in' because you just exited the interstate or 'turn on' inn like a sixties throw back. Works either way." Susan looked nice tonight. She had on Levi's, western boots, a subtle black silk blouse, and a white vest. "Sounds like they have a band!"

The inside of Turn On Inn was a continuation of the exterior design theme. A sign outside the bar read 'Established 1956'. Most of the furniture looked like it was from that same year. It was all worn, ragged, and haphazard – even the hi-top tables that were just squares of plywood attached to 55-gallon drums. A couple of other tables made use of old wooden wire spools from the power company.

Lined with several unmatched bar stools, a well-worn bar extended across the front of the huge room. The bartender was constantly in motion. The backside of the bar had four pool tables and a couple of classic video games. An empty gumball machine stood next to the games.

"Very urban-chic." Susan whispered in my ear.

Along the far wall was a small, slightly raised bandstand. The band was finishing their rendition of an Allman Brothers Band song.

"There's Buddy!" To my surprise, he was playing guitar with the band. Putting away his instrument, he saw me, smiled, and pointed to a long table with several people sitting around, clapping enthusiastically for the band.

"Why didn't you tell me you were playing?" After making introductions to the group, I finally had a chance to ask Buddy my question.

"We're not officially a band. We get together and play on Friday nights. Been doing it so long we're part of the décor. Also, I thought you might not come if you knew I was playing. Most people don't think of me as a lyrical sort." Motioning to the waitress, Buddy took a swig of his beer. "Another round for the table!"

"Hoss is our bass player. He had a serious run in with the Littles before he retired as a Fulton County deputy. He's one tough fellow. Someone stiffed one of the Littles on a drug deal. Who was that, Hoss?" Buddy addressed Hoss, a very stout looking man.

"Barnabas Collins Little. He was named after that vampire in the soap opera Dark Shadows." Hoss had a raspy, smoker's voice. "I was in an unmarked car, parked right there in Buddy's parking lot. The man who stiffed Barnabas stopped to get gas at Buddy's place. Barnabas drove up, stepped out of his car, and shot the man dead while he was pumping gas.

Right there in front of me. I called for backup and tried to arrest him. He put up a hell of a fight. Buddy broke it up by hitting Barnabas in the head with a tire iron.

"They put Barnabas in jail with a forty year sentence. Eighteen months into the sentence, he got shanked. Since then the Littles have hated me. Blame me for it. They're none too happy with Buddy either." Hoss sat back in his chair. Even though he was retired, bald, and a little paunchy in the mid-section, I sure wouldn't want to tangle with him. "Ready for another set?"

Buddy and the band played another set, mostly classic southern rock but they occasionally played songs that were completely out of their genre. They played a reggae version of 'Caught in a Trap' and a country version of 'Gangsta's Paradise' that left the crowd, all twenty of us, laughing.

"Play some Katy Perry!" Susan yelled. She was having a great time, as was I.

Buddy and his band huddled quickly. "We know 'Hot and Cold' but we'll need a female singer."

Susan jumped up and ran onto the small stage. They did a great job considering they didn't know the song well and with a new singer. Susan has a great voice and she knew the words by heart. She really made the song.

With a little prompting, the whole bar gave them a standing ovation.

"You were great!" Giving Susan a hug, I pulled out her chair for her and she collapsed in it laughing, her eyes sparkling.

But all good things have to come to an end.

Bursting through the door came all the bad things in the form of four of the Littles. There was Patch and Jughead who were easily recognizable. They were with two other Littles that I remembered from my visit the previous night. They had pulled Jughead off their party client. I didn't know which soap opera they represented.

"Whooo weeee! Bring on the beers! We're ready to have some fun!" Patch was loud and boisterous. The others were just as loud but less understandable.

Around our table, the mood changed. Everyone was on high alert. We were all familiar with the Littles and knew their presence would only lead to trouble.

"Where's the bartender?" Patch slammed his hand down hard on the bar.

"Yeh. Where's the bartender?" Jughead imitated Patch and slammed his hand on the bar, too. His severely bucked teeth gave his words a more muffled sound and muted the pronunciation. Jughead's version was much less effective audibly but much more frightening visually. He looked mad and the rest of the bunch looked upset.

"She didn't have to go out with that feller tonight. She didn't! I can't keep an eye on him if I'm not there." Jughead was clearly distraught. He was clinching his fists again and the veins on his forehead were pulsating.

"Now, Jughead. Calm down. You know that escorting is part of the service that the Playhouse offers. That feller just needed a date tonight." Patch put his arm around Jughead's shoulder and gave him a consoling pat on the back.

"Someone else should have gone. What about Alexandra?" Jughead looked sharply at Patch.

"Alexandra? She's not as experienced as Lil' Tami. She's only fifteen and just gettin' started. Now calm down. We'll get a few beers in us and pretty soon the night will be over. Tami will be back home and you won't have to worry." Patch was being very comforting to Jughead.

"Where's the damn beers?" Patch whirled around and slammed his fist down on the bar again making the whole platform shake. The bartender quickly gave them each a Pabst. "You were so slow on that beer, go ahead and get us another." Patch turned up his can and swigged down half the beer.

Patch whirled around with a wild, drunken look in his eye and glared at us. "What are ya'll looking at?"

Hoss was up from his seat in a second, which was fine with me. I'd already had my fill of the Littles.

"I'm not quite sure what we're looking at. You're either a bunch of thirsty folks wanting to have a drink or a bunch of thirsty folks wanting to have trouble. If you want a drink, stay at the bar. If you want trouble, you found it." Hoss got right to the point. From his language and demeanor, he seemed to be hoping for a fight.

All four of the Littles headed our way. The men at our table, including myself, stood up in anticipation of the potential problem. I sized up the situation. There were four of them and five of us. They were half our ages but we were experienced. They were crazy and we were mostly sane. It stacked up pretty even.

Standing chest-to-chest, Patch and Hoss squared off. The room went silent for several seconds.

Personally, I had boxed a little in Golden Gloves when I was in college but I had not been in a fight since then. Even then, I was only a mediocre boxer. I was better at taking a blow than delivering one. Sizing up the Little in front of me, I evaluated my ability to take him. I guessed he was in his early twenties, medium build with a strong resemblance to Patch, only without the patch. He had a full head of greasy, dirty blond hair. One noticeable attribute was the large biceps accentuated by the sleeveless shirt. This guy had been seriously working out.

Compared to myself – I was in my early thirties, somewhat past my prime. My auburn hair had a touch of grey but at least I still had most of it. I used to be in great shape – went to the gym every day. That was before my financial debacle. I wasn't fat now but I had certainly lost some muscle tone. My plan was to hit hard and hit fast; I probably didn't have the stamina to do much more than that.

Standing beside me was Buddy, matched with Jughead. However, Jughead had other plans. He changed places with my man so that he squared off with me.

"I thought Pa made it clear to stay out of our business." Jughead gave me a wide grin, showing his yellow, filthy teeth. Even knowing it was coming, I was still unprepared for the stench of his breath.

Bam! A massive, ringing sound made all of us jump and turn towards the source.

Standing in front of the bar was a big, over-weight man in a white t-shirt with an apron tied around his waist. In his hands was a baseball bat, which he had just slammed against the top of one of the hi-top tables. He hit the tabletop again, this time so hard that the top of the tabletop flipped off and knocked over the 55-gallon drum used as its base.

The man then proceeded to beat the 55-gallon drum with the bat until the sides caved in. The sound permeated the bar.

"No more! If you boys want to fight, take it outside and off my property!" The man pointed the bat at all of us. He looked like the cook. Buddy told me later that he was Tiny, the owner.

"I've told you Littles to stay out of my bar! The last time ya'll come in here, you tore the place up so bad it took me a week to put it back together. I want all you Littles out – now! If you ain't out in two seconds, I'm calling the police. Not the Chattahoochee Valley police either but the Georgia State Patrol. I don't think any of you Littles want that." The owner's face was blood red from anger and exertion. Another swing of the bat, or another sentence, would probably give him a heart attack.

The front door burst open and the security man from outside came roaring in with a ball bat at ready. "What's the problem here?"

From my vantage point, I saw Jughead's hand sliding slowly behind his back. He lifted his shirt slightly as he reached for the butt of a gun.

Grabbing his hand and wrenching his arm upward, I moved without thinking. I pushed forward hard against Jughead and knocked him to the floor, ramming my knee into his back. Whipping his pistol from its hiding place and stepping back, I held the gun at ready.

"Step back against the wall and show your hands." I motioned at the Littles with the barrel of the gun. If Jughead had a gun, I assumed the other Littles had guns also.

"Give me the gun, Roger." Hoss gingerly reached his hand out for the gun. "If you're on probation, you don't need to have a gun in your hand, much less shoot anyone."

I handed Hoss the gun.

"It's an automatic. You need to take off the safety for the first shot." Hoss readied the gun and leveled it at the Littles. "Besides, I'm an ex-cop."

"What do you want to do, Tiny?" Hoss addressed the owner. "Shoot them here, call the police, or send them away?"

"Send them away. Don't any of you come back!" Tiny pointed at the door with the bat.

The Littles went out the door. Jughead was the last in line. Before exiting, he stopped and turned towards me. Sneering, he revealed his big, cracked yellow teeth again. "You made me mad."

Turning to Hoss, he held out his hand. "I want my gun back."

"No. I'm keeping it." Hoss kept the gun at ready.

Jughead glared at him but left.

All four Littles clambered into the front seat of the pickup. The rough running truck spit and coughed to life, followed immediately with spinning tires on gravel. The rocks pelted the parked cars and the front of the building. A rock hit one of the windows to the bar and the glass cracked in a spider web pattern.

The bar patrons, other than our table, immediately piled out through the front door.

"Damn. They didn't pay their tabs." The owner shouldered his bat. Looking at us and shaking his head, he went back to his job in the kitchen.

Ejecting the clip, and the round in the chamber, Hoss handed the pistol to me. "It's a 9mm Ruger LC-9. You're going to need it. Get some ammo, learn to use it, keep it handy. This pistol is deadly at close range, not so accurate at a distance, but it makes a hell of a noise!"

We settled our tabs and left the bar.

"Sorry about this, Roger. Jughead is a bad person to have mad at you." Buddy pulled me aside as we approached our cars. He shook my hand, which wasn't needed since my hand was shaking enough by itself. "We all appreciate what you did tonight. It could have ended very badly. Although now, you've made a bad enemy. If you need help, don't hesitate to call me at any time."

"Thanks, Buddy, but it was just a reaction on my part." A reaction I was already regretting. The last thing I needed was more trouble.

Susan was already in the truck. The moonlight overly dramatized the whiteness of her face. She had not spoken since the incident occurred. I climbed into the driver's seat, started the engine, and pulled out of the parking lot.

"What do we do now? We can't afford to move, can't afford rent. You can't get another job. You're on probation and now you have a gun in your pocket." Susan finally spoke. Her tears sparkled in the dashboard lights and she quickly wiped them away. "I don't want to lose you – not now. Everything seemed like it was turning to the better. Why didn't you just stay out of it?"

"He was reaching for a gun. I had no choice. If he had pulled that gun, there's no telling what he would have done. He's a deranged person and might have shot us all." Pulling the gun out of my pocket, I stuffed it under the seat.

"He's not deranged, he's inbred. My dad raised horses and that's what he called the inbred horses – jugheads. They had the same big head and stupid attitude like our Jughead. They were never quite right. They can hurt you simply because they are so stupid." Talking seemed to help Susan. She lifted her head and looked me straight in the eye. "We can deal with it. I'm tired of us being pushed around – especially by a bunch of inbred country hicks."

"I'm tired of being pushed around too, but it may get very unpleasant and nasty." Although surprised that Susan wanted to make a stand, I was glad.

"We're not moving. This is our last chance. From here, there's nowhere else to go." Susan said it vehemently and with finality. "We are here to stay."

"That's quite a statement from the eternal optimist." I attempted a smile.

"Just because I'm an optimist doesn't mean that I don't get angry, pissed off, outraged! I'm stubborn, too. We stuck together through your mess – I mean our mess – and stayed out of jail. We will get through this. Those morons aren't running me out. And that's one stubborn, pissed off, OPTIMIST talking!" Susan punctuated her statement by firmly crossing her arms.

We were about a quarter of a mile from our house. Glancing in the rearview mirror, I saw headlights approaching rapidly. The car closed the gap until it was just inches from our bumper, then it stayed there – no more, no less.

"We have company." It was a useless statement since the headlights illuminated the inside of the car. I wished I had not pushed the gun so far under the seat and that I had reloaded it.

Just before we reached our house, the car hit its blue lights and siren. It was the police.

Pulling into the driveway, the police car parked behind us and left its blue lights flashing. Of course, it was Chattahoochee Valley.

"Step out of the car please." The police officer tapped on my window. I recognized the voice of Deputy Justus.

"Seems you've been busy, Roger. I have a complaint that you stole a gun and were brandishing it at the Turn On Inn. You know that's a violation of your probation agreement. This could land you in jail for a very long time." The deputy leaned back against his car, lit a cigarette, and blew the smoke in my direction. The smoke and the flashing blue lights gave his face a menacing glow.

"I thought Turn On Inn was outside the Chattahoochee Valley jurisdiction. Besides, there was a Fulton County deputy there who took my name and information." It was only a bit of a stretch on the story.

"Yeah. Hoss. I believe he's retired. Problem is I have four people ready to take out a complaint against you. Now, why don't you come with me? C'mon. We'll go have a talk with them and sort this thing out." Deputy Justus opened the back seat of the patrol car and motioned me inside.

"Honey?" Susan interrupted before I moved. "You have a phone call. It's the State Patrol. They want to come out and take a statement from you about the incident at the bar tonight. Hoss reported it to them." Exiting the car and walking towards us, Susan held the phone out to me.

"Hello." I took the phone.

"Just say 'Yes sir. I was there.'." Hoss was on the other end.

"Yes sir. I was there." I was glad to hear his gruff voice.

"Now. Tell me that you're home and you will be waiting for us to arrive." Hoss kept his voice in a hushed tone to prevent the Deputy from overhearing.

"Yes. I'll be home and will wait for your Trooper to arrive. Fifteen minutes? Sure, no problem. Thank you." I hung up the phone.

"I guess you heard. I need to wait around since the patrol unit is already on the way. Sorry I can't go with you." Saved by Hoss' call, I waited for the deputy's next move.

"Maybe some other time then." Deputy Justus closed the back door to his cruiser and sat down in the driver's seat. "I suggest that you rinse out your mouth before the Trooper arrives. I smell the beer on your breath. It would be bad to get arrested for drinking and driving. You don't have to thank me. Neighbors watch out for each other that way. It would do you good to remember that.

"Mrs. Multry, you're even prettier than Jughead said. You know, he's quite smitten with you. He was hoping to have a dance with you tonight before all the trouble started." The deputy nodded at Susan but lingered too long with his eyes.

Turning off the blue lights and putting the cruiser in reverse, he hesitated before backing out of the driveway. "You might want to check out 'LilTamisPlayhouse.com'. Might be something there of interest to you." With that, he backed out of the driveway, squealing the tires of the cruiser as he pulled away.

Susan and I watched his taillights disappear into the Little's driveway.

"That was a lucky call from Hoss – just in the nick of time. I don't know what would have happened if he'd taken me to the Little's house." Susan and I turned around and walked towards the house.

"He didn't call. I called him. When I saw it was the Chattahoochee Valley Police, I had to come up with something. I'd like my cell phone back please." Susan held out her hand.

"Brilliant! He sure didn't want to be around if the State Troopers were coming. He high-tailed it out of here! Thank you." I gave Susan a kiss on her cheek.

"I told you, I don't want to lose you now." She gave me a little shove. "What do you think he meant about the website?"

"We'll check it out first thing in the morning. For now, let's hit the sack. It's been a long day." I had been in a fight, stopped by the police, and threatened with jail time; I wanted this day to end.

Chapter 9

Saturday. It used to be my day. Catch up on some emails, run a few errands, and maybe have a dip in the pool in the afternoon with a fruity cocktail. Susan and I would then be off to dinner at a nice restaurant, have a bottle or two of wine, and enjoy a nice evening overlooking the city from our living room.

Saturday. Now I can't even sleep in late. To meet the terms of our rental agreement, I had to put in time on house improvements to cover the bulk of our rent.

Shaking my head, I looked at the sad set of tools in the toolshed. Rusty hand tools, a dicey looking weed eater (at least there was one), and a push mower that was probably twenty-five years old. I pulled out the mower, filled it with gas, and pulled the starting rope – and pulled –

and pulled. I pulled it at least twice for each year of its life.

The mower finally came to life with a puff of blue smoke. The smoke thickened whenever the mower went through tough patches of grass. I had to go over those spots several times to get the grass even. The blade definitely needed sharpening. Still, when I finished the front yard, it looked much better.

The back yard was a different story. The grass was too tall, thick, and tough for either the mower or the weed eater. I went back to the shed and retrieved the sling blade, the manual predecessor to the weed eater.

Swish. Swish. Swish. Swinging the sling blade back and forth, I soon found a comfortable rhythm. I managed to stay out of jail only to find myself doing the same job as the county prisoner road crews.

"Come in and get some iced tea!" Susan called from the kitchen window. Soaked with sweat, covered with dirt and grass clippings, I needed a break. She threw a dry t-shirt to me through the open window. "Take off that shirt before you come in."

"That's good tea." In the kitchen, I drank half the glass in one gulp.

"Let's look at Lil' Tami's web site." Susan had the laptop sitting on the kitchen table. It was one of the miscellaneous luxury items they let us keep since it was older technology and not worth much. Susan called up LilTamisPlayhouse.com.

"Here it is. It's a colorful site. There are some pictures of Lil' Tami in her cutoffs. She really shouldn't pull those shorts up so high like that, it looks painful." Susan clicked through some other pages on the site. "These pictures must have been made inside their party room. There's a bunch of pictures of girls all over people on the couch. It doesn't look like a hardcore porn site, just revealing. Here's a section called 'Topless of the Night' for people to contribute their own topless pictures…"

Susan's voice trailed off and her face turned pale. She slid the laptop over for me to see.

There, under a section called 'Hot Girl Next Door', was Susan's picture, and she was topless. The pictures were a little grainy but there was no doubt it was Susan. There were numerous pictures of her, all taken while she was in the bathroom of this house! There were before shower and after shower pictures, drying her hair, combing her hair, and even one of her putting on deodorant.

Taken from a distance and framed by the bathroom window, whoever took the pictures took them from somewhere in the backyard. The caption under the photo album read, 'Come by and you might meet this hot lady!'.

I jumped up and ran to the bathroom window, scanning the backyard for a likely location to hide a shutterbug. Susan was still in a state of shock.

"I just haven't put up the curtains in the bathroom. It's so wooded out back, no houses around, it seemed private. I just didn't get around to the curtains yet." Susan stood at the door, staring blankly. She pointed out the window. "There it is."

Looking where she pointed, at first I saw nothing. Then, I saw a reflection like sunlight bouncing off a piece of glass. The flicker of light was along the tree line in the back of the yard. The tree was on the other side of the remnants of a fence, long overgrown with thick grass, weeds, and small sapling trees. I saw the flash again. This time it was moving lower. There was someone in the tree with a camera and it looked like he was climbing down.

I ran outside and grabbed the sling blade on my way across the backyard. Fighting my way through the undergrowth, I saw a figure jump the last few feet down the tree. He was still too far away to be clearly recognizable but I would bet money it was Jughead.

I fiercely beat my way through the tangled growth with the sling blade. I was breathing hard and sweating but my anger kept me going. Climbing through the last bit of briars, I finally reached the woods at the edge of the pasture.

As I expected, our Peeping Tom was long gone. I didn't see anyone. Not used to running, especially on such a hot day, I bent over sucking wind. My need for oxygen quickly quelled my anger.

Hearing a sound behind me, I whirled with the sling blade raised at ready. It was Susan. I dropped the blade.

"You…surprised…me." I managed to wheeze out.

"Thought you might need help." Susan held up the handgun she retrieved from the truck. "It's loaded and ready to go."

"Whoever it was is gone. Took me too long to get here." Although still sweating profusely, I was breathing a little more normally. I pointed to a platform in the tree. "Look up there."

"A deer stand? They were taking pictures of me from a deer stand?" Susan wasn't outraged so much as trying to make sense of it.

"Look at the ladder leading up to the platform. Looks like it's been used a lot lately." I showed her the trampled undergrowth around the tree. "There's scrapes on the tree bark from the trips up and down the ladder. I don't think they were hunting deer in the middle of the summer."

"Did they do this just to get even with us for last night? Do you want the gun?" Susan flicked on the safety of the gun and offered it to me.

"No. You keep it. You obviously know more about it than I do. Guess you learn a lot of things growing up on a farm. I'll stick to my mighty sling blade." I lifted the sling blade into the air and gave it a shake. I felt safer with her having a gun. "I don't think it was because of last night though. They've probably been taking pictures since we moved in. It looks like the trail winds through the woods there. I bet it comes out down the road near the Little's house."

"What can we do about the pictures? We have to get them taken down." Susan pocketed the gun.

"Talking to the Littles is out. If I show up there, I'm not sure what would happen. Deputy Justus certainly had plans for me last night. We might be able to contact their website host but we'll probably have to get a lawyer." I really was not sure what to do.

"We can probably get a free consultation with a lawyer. Otherwise, I don't know how we can afford one. Maybe no one will see the pictures until then." Susan, always the optimist.

Chapter 10

"There's nothing we can do without a lawyer." Susan sighed as she served up a Saturday night dinner of hot dogs, Tater Tots, and two cold beers. She'd spent the afternoon researching how to get her pictures removed from Lil' Tami's site. "The only other option is to convince the Littles to remove the pictures. We know that won't happen."

"Tomorrow is Sunday so we can't do anything. Monday morning I have to see my probation officer." I was tired. After putting up the curtains in the bathroom, I immersed myself in the yard work. Sweating helped work off some of my anger. "I'll have to ask Buddy for some time off."

"You need to make money. I can go to the lawyer for the consultation. I know what I want to have happen. We need to know how much it will cost to get their help. I'll need the truck though because I want to start right away." Susan put some mayonnaise on her hot dog, a taste I had never acquired. "I'll also need to look for a job next week."

"We'll need another car when you go back to work." My mind automatically did a few calculations. "We might be able to buy a plastic model car but that's about it. Whoever said 'you have to spend money to make money' probably had money in the first place."

After we finished dinner, we took our beers outside. I found a couple of old lawn chairs and we sat under the trees in the front yard for a while. It was cooler than inside the house and the fresh cut lawn smelled nice.

"The Littles are partying early tonight. Is that Waylon they're playing?" The music was blaring, cars pulled into their driveway with some having to park on the side of the road. Occasionally, I caught a whiff of their barbeque.

"If it wasn't so hot, I'd go back inside. I get angry all over again when I think about them. But to answer your question, it's not Waylon; it's Hank Williams, Jr." Susan was the music connoisseur.

A car left the Littles, driving in our direction. As they went by, the driver blew his horn and the entire carload hooted and yelled, waving at us. There were a couple of wolf calls thrown in.

The same occurred when the next car left and drove by. When the first car returned, probably from a beer run, they slowed down, blew their horn again, and repeated their jeers. One of the men pulled up his t-shirt and bared his chest at us.

"They found the website." Susan's eyes widened.

"Do you want me to call the State Patrol? They're disturbing the peace." My voice belied my confidence that they would get involved.

"What? And have Deputy Philip Kiriakis from Days of Our Lives come and take you off to jail? I don't think so." Susan got up and went straight to bed. Putting in a DVD, she turned the volume up to drown out the sounds.

The horn blowing and catcalls continued into the night. Despite the heat, Susan pulled her pillow over her head. I heard her crying a couple of times.

I tried to sleep throughout the night but to no avail. Having put us, and especially Susan, into this position, I felt helpless in finding a way to correct it. Each day mired us deeper and deeper into the muck with no way out.

Along with the arrival of Sunday morning, came a welcomed silence. The party next door was over, for now. Susan was finally sound asleep so I did my best not to wake her.

I poured myself some coffee and went outside to enjoy this brief period of solitude. I heard a ringing bell and saw the now familiar unicycle and white helmet coming down the road. I didn't say anything this time, but Yuri still shot me a bird.

The sound of a puttering truck caught my attention. It was Pa Little.

"Yuri, you get on back to the house and get ready for Sunday school! You don't want to make everybody late!" Leaning out the window, Pa Little motioned at the boy.

Yuri rang the bell twice, did an about face with the unicycle, and headed back towards his house. I noted that he did not shoot Pa a bird. Pa Little pulled his truck into my driveway. The morning's moment of solitude became a fleeting memory – or maybe it had been a delusion all along.

"Morning, Roger. Glad you're up. I want to talk at you for a bit." I knew that Pa Little's friendliness contradicted his intentions but I was glad no one else was with him.

"I'm glad you came by, Mr. Little. I need to talk to you, too." I stuck to my minor revolt by not calling him 'Pa'.

"You go first, Roger. You seem a mite heated up about something." Getting out and walking to the back of the truck, Pa opened a cooler, pulled out an ice-cold Pabst, and offered it to me. "Hair of the dog."

"No sir. It's still early for me."

"Suit yourself. Now, tell me what's on your mind." Popping the top on the beer, Pa pulled a saltshaker from the bib of his overalls and sprinkled some onto the top of the can.

"It's about the web site for Lil' Tami's Playhouse. Did you know that someone took pictures of my wife, topless, and posted them on the site?" I was sure he knew but I was trying to be diplomatic.

"Yeah. Them kids!" He shook his head with a wry smile, as if a three year old said something cute. "You can't ever tell what they'll do."

"Well, it's pretty upsetting! Susan doesn't want those pictures available for anyone to see. We want them taken down!" I was holding firm.

"I asked 'em. Stanley said your wife agreed to it. Even seemed to be posing. Stanley has a bit of a crush on her, you know. He fancies himself a lady's man. I'll tell them to get those pictures off today." Pa frowned as if truly offended that his kindred would lie to him. "I can't do that stuff myself. Don't know the first thing about computers. You check though and tell me if the pictures aren't removed."

"Thank you, Mr. Little." I still had my doubts.

"Now, I need to ask you a favor. Give Stanley the gun back." Pa Little stuck out his hand and made the shape of a gun like he was shooting at me. "Stanley's all in an uproar about that gun. It was his favorite. Giving the gun back might smooth things over, especially if you apologize."

"I'm not going to apologize. I stopped him from shooting someone. You should be thanking me." I was in disbelief at his request.

"Naw. He wouldn't have shot anyone. He just wanted to get his way. Give him back the gun and apologize. Believe me, you'll be much happier not having Stanley mad at you." Pa Little took another sip of his beer. "Awww. That's good."

"Sorry, Mr. Little. I can't do it." Giving the gun back wasn't a reasonable option.

"I understand Roger. If you can't, you can't." He turned to get back in the truck but stopped. "Now, what was it you wanted me to do when I get home?"

"Take my wife's pictures off your web site." I saw where this was going. No apology, no removal.

"Oh, yeah. Right. I forgot. Hope I can remember when I get home. An apology though, that might help my memory. You think about what I said – but don't think too long." He pulled out of the driveway and drove off towards the Little's domain.

I certainly thought about Pa Little's words. Trying to rationalize his request, I saw

Jughead's point. After all, it is his gun, so that partially justifies giving it back. The apology though, that was something I didn't want to do. It would set a bad precedent with the Littles.

Still, if it got the pictures removed, it would be worth it.

I went into the house and found Jughead's gun on the nightstand next to Susan's side of the bed. Retrieving the gun, I went to my truck and headed for the Littles. Getting this over quickly was my goal.

As I approached the Littles driveway, two of their teenagers were playing Frisbee in the middle of the road. I didn't recognize them but was sure they represented some soap opera. A car approaching from the other direction beeped its horn and the boys cleared the road. As soon as the car passed, they went back to their game.

There were several cars in the Littles' yard, a few chickens scratching around, and quite a few people just hanging around. Two men were working under the hood of an old police interceptor Crown Victoria, three or four were chopping wood, others were talking in groups, a few women were shucking corn under the shade of the trees with their babies playing on the ground in front of them.

As I exited the truck, the dogs came slinking around. They walked around me with their heads hung low, emitting a grumbling growl from the depths of their throats.

"Get on out of here." Pa Little came from the side door of the house, letting the screen door slam behind him. The dogs immediately dispersed. "Glad you dropped by to see us, Roger."

"I thought about what you said. If the pictures will be removed, I'll give back the gun and apologize to Jug – uh – Stanley." I briefly stumbled on Jughead's natural name.

"Great." Pa walked back to the door of the house and yelled inside. "Stanley! Patch! Ya'll come outside. Roger has something he wants to say."

Jughead came out the door along with Patch and their two companions from the bar. They all sneered and glared at me, expressing their dislike.

"Hello Stanley. I wanted to bring back your gun and apologize for our misunderstanding at Turn On Inn." There. I felt I had done what Pa Little asked. I looked over at him for confirmation. Pa nodded at Jughead.

"You didn't shoot it did you?" Jughead expertly removed the clip, ejected the round from the chamber, and smelled it for recent gunpowder. "I don't like anybody to shoot my guns."

"No. I didn't shoot it. It's just like it was. All the bullets and everything."

"Good. I didn't like you taking it from me. You sorry you took it?" Jughead reloaded the gun and stuck it in the back of his belt.

"Yes, Stanley. Of course. We're neighbors. I wouldn't want to make you mad. I just didn't want the argument to go too far. Someone, even you, might have gotten hurt." Swallowing the apology was more difficult than I expected.

"I wouldn't have shot anyone but you hurt my back when you knocked me down." Faster than I would have expected possible, Jughead hit me on the left side of my face.

Caught off-guard, I stumbled sideways but managed to stay on my feet. One of the Littles caught and steadied me. I thought he was helping but he and Patch pinned my arms behind my back.

Jughead stepped over, punched me twice in the belly, and then hit me again in the mouth. I felt the blood trickling down my chin. Jughead drew back to hit me again.

"That's enough." Pa Little spoke softly and Jughead stopped in mid-swing. "He is our neighbor and he did apologize."

"But Pa! He took my gun and knocked me down. He has to be taught a lesson." Jughead was mad and he kicked at the dirt with the toe of his boot.

"Let him go." Pa Little spoke tersely. My captors released my arms and I fell to the ground. "I want those pictures of his wife taken down from the website."

"Pa! Those are my favorites. A lot of people have been looking at them. You should see the number of hits." Jughead was upset, like a child getting his favorite candy taken away.

"You heard me." Pa turned and walked back in the house.

I was breathing better following the punches to my stomach but I was still on my hands and knees, spitting blood. Jughead stepped on my hand and then kicked me in the ribs with his steel-toed boot, knocking me onto my side.

"That's for having to take the pictures down." Jughead leaned over and whispered in my ear. "Remember, I still have a bunch of them pictures on my camera – some you haven't seen."

Jughead and the rest of his group walked away. They had such disdain for me that they didn't bother to look back.

I heaved myself upright, stumbled to my truck, and headed back to my house. I accomplished what I set out to accomplish but I felt no elation.

At the house, I cleaned myself up as much as possible. The nasty cut on my lip swelled up like a botched Botox treatment. The tissue around my eye turned a nice shade of purple and even the eyeball itself was very red. I didn't think my ribs were broken but they were severely bruised and tender. It hurt when I breathed. My hand was sore, scraped and the knuckles already stiff and swollen.

I returned to the kitchen, poured a cup of coffee with my good hand, and sat down at the table. I knew it was too soon but I opened the laptop and checked Lil' Tami's website. The pictures were still there. There seemed to be more pictures than the last time we looked and with more risqué captions.

"What are you doing? Why are you looking at those pictures? Are you sneaking a look at me – or at Tami? That is sick!" I didn't hear Susan come into the kitchen. "And what happened to your face?"

"I was just checking to see if the pictures had been taken down." Based on her reaction, she must have thought I was browsing her topless pictures on the internet. "I'm not browsing your pictures. Pa Little came by and we made a deal. If I gave back the gun and apologized, they would take down the pictures."

"And your face?" Susan's expression was pure skepticism.

"Well. Jughead felt that an apology wasn't enough. He gave my ribs a pretty good workout, too." I lifted my shirt and showed her my bruises.

"Now I believe you. Do we call the police?" Susan refreshed the page but the pictures were still there. "I look kind of cute in that one."

"No. I don't want any police trouble. It would be turned on me some way. Especially if it came out that I was in possession of a gun." I flipped back a couple of pages and pointed to a different picture. "That one is my favorite."

"There are over twenty pictures." While Susan cleaned and treated my wounds, I checked the pages, hoping to see something removed. Then, there was an update. "Hey! It's down to ten pictures!"

"Did they say they would only take down half?" Susan was constantly hitting 'Refresh.'

We checked the site every few minutes throughout the afternoon and evening but there were no more updates – it stayed at ten pictures.

"I going to talk to a lawyer about the pictures tomorrow but I'll need the truck." Susan sighed as we turned in for the night. All the pictures remained on the site. "I'll look for a job, too."

"After the probation officer in the morning, I'll come by and pick you up so you can have the truck in the afternoon. Maybe Buddy will bring me home." I turned off the light and turned up the sound on the television to drown out the party from down the street.

Chapter 11

———————

"Mr. Multry. I'm not quite sure what to do with you." My probation officer sat back in his chair and looked at me over the top of his reading glasses.

"What do you mean?" My Monday morning visit with the probation officer wasn't starting out as well as I hoped.

"I have two reports from two different police agencies." He leaned forward, shuffled some papers, and found the one he wanted. "Here, as reported by the Chattahoochee Valley police department, you were reported to have been involved in an altercation at an establishment called the 'Turn On Inn.' No arrests were made but a gun was involved.

"In another report, from a retired Fulton County deputy sheriff, you are commended in helping to stop an altercation at the same establishment." He flipped the papers across the desk for me to read.

"That is true. I assisted the Fulton County deputy when a bar customer pulled a gun." I wasn't sure which way to take the conversation but I thought it best to downplay my involvement. "The deputy did most everything. I just held the man for a moment. The Chattahoochee Valley police weren't involved."

"Is that how you got that black eye and busted lip?" He was eying my face.

"Yes." That seemed to be a better explanation than the truth.

The probation officer thought for a moment before he spoke. "I want to remind you that any trouble with the law will likely land you in prison for a very long time. You are not to have contact with firearms, you are not to cavort with known criminals, you are not to get arrested. In your case, you are not to take any job in the financial industry. Any contrary acts on your part will be considered a violation of the terms of your probation – possibly resulting in jail time. Understood?"

I nodded my head. I had signed a similar agreement.

"Okay. See you next Monday." He motioned me out the door.

As I neared my truck in the courthouse parking lot, there was Tami. She was leaning back against the front fender, smoking a cigarette.

"What are you doing here?" I looked around quickly to see if any of her kinfolk were around.

"Saw your truck, so I told Patch to go on home, I'd get a ride with you. Told you we could carpool." Tami took a last draw from the cigarette, tossed it to the ground, and squashed it out with the toe of her boot.

"Is that what you wear to see a probation officer?" Her attire looked more fitting for a party than the courthouse. She had on her trademark cut-off jeans, a white tank top, cowboy boots, and deep red lipstick.

"You mean Herb? He doesn't mind. He used to come by Fannie's all the time. I gave him so many lap dances that he should be in the frequent riders' program. We have an agreement now. I even get a tip for my visit." She pulled a twenty out of her bra and showed it to me. "Now, let's get going."

"This isn't a good time, Tami. I have to get home and then go to work. Plus Susan needs the truck." Taking her home did not sound like a good idea in any form or fashion.

"I thought you might want to talk about taking those other ten pictures of your wife off the website. Besides, it would only take two or three extra minutes to drop me off at my house. Patch will be awfully angry if he has to come back to get me." Tami was already at the truck door with her hand on the handle.

"Okay. Just this once but you have to have your own ride next time." I didn't have much choice.

Resigning myself to the situation, I unlocked the truck. Tami quickly slipped inside and slid over to the center of the bench seat, uncomfortably close to me. I felt the warmth of her bare leg and I moved mine away a bit.

"You shy?" Tami knew she was making me uncomfortable and she played the moment up. Taking a bottle of lotion from her bag, she squirted some onto her hand and proceeded to rub it on her legs – ankles to thighs. It had the scent of vanilla and strawberries. "This doesn't bother you does it? I wouldn't want to get you in trouble with your wife."

"No, it doesn't bother me but if you moved over you would have more room." I was uncomfortable. She was forward, aggressive, wild, and untamed. I sure didn't need any trouble – no trouble from her, no trouble from the Littles, no trouble from the law, and especially no trouble from Susan. "Look. Yes. It does bother me. You need to move over to the passenger side of the truck."

"My legs are so soft and smooth. Want to feel them." Tami gave no indication of moving away, as if she didn't even hear me. She pushed her leg harder against mine.

"No. If you don't move over, I'll stop the truck and you'll have to walk home." I had no idea what else to do.

"I'll tell you what. You want the pictures of your wife taken off the website, right?" Tami looked at me with a sly twinkle in her eye. "If you'll rub my legs and feel how smooth they are, I'll take down the rest of the pictures."

"I can't do that! That wouldn't be right for anyone – especially after everything Susan and I have been through. I've never cheated on her and I won't start now." Unfortunately, my concerns about riding with Tami were coming true. Her alluring fragrance did not help matters.

"Nobody will know. Just you and me. If you don't do it, I might have to tell Pa and Jughead that you did anyway." This time she gave me an outright smile. "You know Pa would be mad, more from a business perspective. He says we don't do nothin' for free. But Jughead…"

Tami shook her head and clucked her cheek. "Jughead would make that little tussle yesterday look like a 'howdy-do'. He don't like you already and if he thought you put your hand on me – well, there's no telling what he would do to you." With that, she took my hand and placed it on her leg.

She was right. Her legs were soft and smooth. I briefly lost myself in their silky smoothness. She pulled my hand up higher on her thigh and I did not resist. Feeling guilty, I pulled my hand away quickly.

"There. That wasn't so bad, was it? I'd like a little more, maybe next time, but that will do for now." Tami patted my lap. "Looks like it got your attention."

"You'll take the pictures down?"

"Sure Honey. I said I would. And this will be our little secret." Tami finished rubbing the lotion on her legs.

"You should slide over. I don't want your family, or Susan, seeing you sitting so close to me." I motioned for her to slide over. Tami did so grudgingly.

Riding past our house, I didn't see Susan in the yard, which was a relief. I pulled into the Littles' driveway. As usual, members of the group were outside, including Jughead.

"Bye, Sweetie. Remember our secret." Tami got out, closed the door, and blew me a kiss through the window.

"Remember our deal. You'll take the pictures down." I didn't want another trick like Pa Little's.

"Don't worry. I'm on my way now." Tami turned on the heel of her boot and twitched towards the house.

"What secret? I don't like secrets!" Jughead asked Tami. However, he was walking straight towards my truck.

Quickly putting the truck in reverse, I backed out of the drive and headed towards my house.

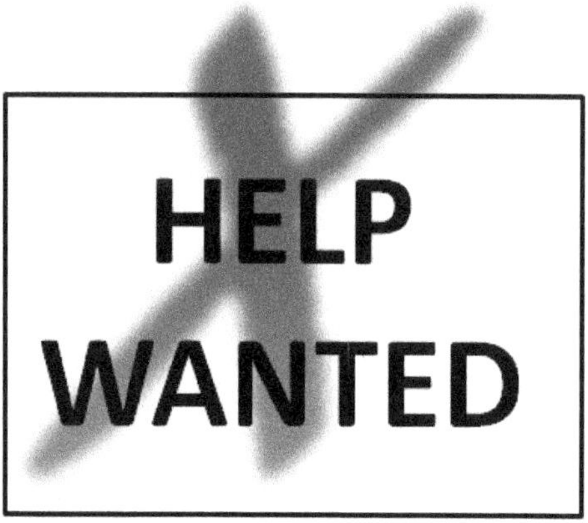
HELP
WANTED

Chapter 12

"What were you doing with Lil' Tami in the truck?" Susan might not have been in the yard but she saw me go by from the kitchen window.

"I gave her a ride home from the probation office. She was pushy about it and she had already sent Patch home. I didn't want to make them mad again. I was trapped." It was the truth but I still felt dirty. "It also gave me a chance to ask her about the website. She said she would take down the rest of the pictures."

"What made her decide that?" Susan was digging deeper and there was a bite to her words.

"She was going to anyway. She just didn't get a chance to finish taking them all down." It was almost the truth. I didn't see a reason to tell her more.

"So, you and Lil' Tami are now friends? You give her rides home and chat her up about your wife's nude pictures?" Susan was getting angrier the longer we talked about it.

"Let's check the website." Susan pulled over the laptop. "It's down to five pictures."

"She said she would take them all down. That was the deal." I reached over and refreshed the screen.

"What deal is that?" Susan snapped a look at me.

"The deal, yes, the deal. The deal was taking her home. If I took her home, she would get rid of the pictures." Another stretch. I was in deep and getting deeper.

Before Susan asked another question, we heard the now familiar chugging and puffing of the Little's pickup. The wheels ground to a stop on the gravel outside.

"Roger! Mr. Multry! Come outside. I got a question for you." It was Jughead.

Susan and I went outside. Lil' Tami was in the passenger seat of the truck and two other boys were in the back. Jughead was clearly upset.

"What's wrong, Stanley?" I was leery of the situation. The last time I spoke to Jughead, he roughed me up.

"What went on with you and Tami? She said something about keeping a secret. I don't like secrets. I want you to tell me what she meant." Jughead rushed towards me.

"I don't know what you're talking about. I don't have a secret with Tami." My glance shifted from Jughead to Tami.

"I told him, but he doesn't believe me. He gets crazy with jealousy." Tami spoke more nonchalantly than with genuine concern. She sat in the truck, filing her nails.

"She said you rubbed her legs! Is that true? You didn't do any more?" Jughead was red in the face. His veins were pulsing on his forehead.

"I told you that's all he did, Stanley! He didn't even try to do anything more. I think there's something wrong with him." Tami gave Jughead an exasperated look and rolled her eyes.

"That's it. Nothing more! I just gave her a ride home." I glanced over at Susan. She clearly did not share the Little's view of leg touching. I had a feeling there would be a discussion later.

"If you ever touch her again – I'll make you regret the day you ever came to this town. Ask about Barry. You just ask her about Barry." Jughead pointed at Tami.

"Who's Barry?" I looked over at Tami and she just flipped her hand as if to throw away the subject.

"Oh, he's the guy that lived here before ya'll. He was going to take me away, show me the beach and the city. Blah, blah. But Jughead caught him." Tami rolled her eyes again.

"You damn right I caught him. He and she were getting ready to leave. I shoved his head through the car window and then rubbed his face in the glass. Gave him a free ride out of town. Tell them what happened next." Jughead looked at Tami and nodded his head towards us.

"Nobody saw Barry again." Tami spat the words at Jughead.

"That's right. Nobody saw Barry again. That's where that furniture came from in that house of yours. It was Barry's. Don't worry though. He's not coming back for it." Jughead looked directly at me and pointed a knuckled finger. "You better keep away from Tami – or you'll disappear."

Jughead got back in the truck and the vehicle lurched forward, spraying dirt and gravel over Susan, me, and the front of the house. Running over our lawn chairs, he slid sideways into the road and huffed away.

I turned to say something to Susan but she held up her hand and stopped me.

"Move your stuff into the other bedroom. After standing by you through the worst times of our life, losing everything we own, forced to live next door to crazy people – after all that, I stayed by you. But this – this is unforgivable. Is that what you want? Do you want her or do you want me?

"Either way, you're in a pickle. If you touch her, Jughead will beat you up. If you touch me, I'll beat you up." With that, Susan turned and went back into the house, slamming the front door behind her.

She immediately came back out with her pocketbook in hand. "Get in the truck. I have to take you to work and then look for a job."

Spending the afternoon at the shop was a relief. I did a head gasket job on an old Impala. It was a hot, greasy job. Buddy was busy out front with gas and parts so there wasn't much time for talking. That was fine with me.

Susan picked me up at closing time. She was so mad when she dropped me off; I would not have been surprised if she didn't come back at all. When I got in the truck, her eyes were red and she had been crying.

"Don't even think I'm crying about us! It seems I'm the wrong kind of people to get work around here." She gave me an angry look.

"What happened?" I saw that her tears were tears of anger.

"I interviewed for a cashier's job at Piggly Wiggly and it went well. Just when the Head Cashier was going to offer me the job, one of her co-workers came over, whispered in her ear, and left. The Head Cashier looked at me and said, 'Mrs. Multry, we're a family business here. We can't offer you a job. It seems that you have some rather revealing pictures on the internet. Maybe you should apply at Lil' Tami's Playhouse.' Then she showed me the door.

"The same thing happened at the bank. They were more subtle but I heard them whispering. I can't get a job in this town!" Susan was tearing up again.

"It'll blow over, Honey. We'll work it out ---." I reached over to rub her on the shoulder but she knocked my hand away.

"Don't even think that I'm not still mad at you. This doesn't change anything." She drove in silence the rest of the way home.

Jubal Little

Chapter 13

———————

The next few days were miserable, even by my new standards of misery. The second bedroom that I moved into was still half-full of our unpacked boxes from the move. There was furniture in the room, which I now knew was 'Barry's', whoever that was. This room was even hotter than our bedroom. The windows had been painted shut and I could not pry them open. I'd have to add another item to my list of chores.

"I'm in a bad spot with Susan and everything I do just seems to get me in deeper. I've only known the Littles for a week and what was left of my life is already wrecked." Working at the shop was not a relief from the heat but it was a relief from the tension at the house. I told Buddy what happened.

"The Littles affect a lot of people that way and you don't even know the half of it. Them and their inbred bunch have pretty much done what they wanted for a long time. Pa Little is bad but they say his father was even worse and his grandfather was a terror. I doubt if there's been a branch on their family tree since before the Civil War." Buddy was wiping down and putting away his tools. We were cleaning up for the day.

"During the Civil War, Jubal Little was the head of the Little clan. They say there were close to a thousand Littles living in this area then, all kinfolk. Jubal didn't take any sides during the war. He was a true hater. Yankee or Rebel, North or South, Black or White, he didn't care. If they weren't a Little, he hated them.

"When Sherman made his march through Georgia, Jubal put together his own army to protect the Little's land. Sherman's army wiped out pretty near all the Littles. They lost a lot of land but Jubal survived. They even owned that land where you're staying.

"He rebuilt the family and was even stricter about not allowing outsiders into the clan. They've carried on that tradition since then. They made a few exceptions but not many. The whole clan has to agree on an outsider.

"The Littles will do anything to get by, except hold a regular paying job – moonshine, drugs, stolen goods, prostitution; they're a one-stop-shop for illegal activity." Buddy closed up the tool chest.

"If everybody knows it, why don't they turn them in to the law?" I squirted some Gojo on my hands in an attempt to remove some of the grease.

"Folks in this part of the country don't like outsiders butting into their affairs. They don't trust them – especially the law. They pretty much stay to themselves. They might not like the Littles and they may be afraid of the Littles, but they're not going to go against the Littles. Besides, if all the Littles weren't put in jail, the remaining ones would most certainly seek revenge." Buddy walked into the office, opened the door on an old refrigerator, and tossed me a beer.

"Do you know anything about this 'Barry' fellow that Jughead mentioned, or rather, used to threaten me?"

"First, understand that Lil' Tami is bad news – they're all bad news but Tami is real bad news. She can turn on the charm. She can manipulate a man and make him think that he's the only person in the world but all the time, she's working a plan. That's what she did to Barry.

"Barry lived in the house that you're in now. He used to go to Turn On Inn and hang out with us but then he fell in with Tami. He went to Lil' Tami's Playhouse parties almost every night. Tami convinced him that she wanted to run away with him, to get away from the rest of the clan. Barry had a little money from a settlement and that's what Tami really wanted.

"She convinced him to sneak away with her. I think she figured to get his money afterwards. But, the thought of Tami leaving, even to score a deal, was more than Jughead's jealously could tolerate. When he caught them about to leave, he went berserk on Barry. Barry hasn't been seen since." Buddy opened his desk drawer, fumbled inside for a second, and pulled out a set of keys.

"That old Buick Regal out there was his. It has been sitting there for six months and nobody's claimed it. I replaced the window in it. It looks like crap and runs like shit but you can drive it if you want." Buddy tossed me the keys.

"What if somebody comes by and claims it?" I was only a little hesitant.

"Well, you're already using Barry's house and furniture; you might as well drive his car." Buddy climbed into his '50 Ford and roared off.

I walked over to the Buick and looked at it a little closer. It was so run down that I thought it was a parts car. It may have been silver at one time but now, covered in a coat of rust, the color no longer mattered. The cloth interior was worn, torn, and dirty. It looked like blood stains on the driver's seat. The good news is that, despite a puff of smoke from the exhaust, the engine ran reasonably well.

Just as I was pulling out of the parking spot, Lil' Tami pulled up in the Little's truck and blocked the path of my car.

"Hey, Honey! You been avoiding me?" Tami hopped out of the truck in her usual cutoffs and cowboy boots.

"Look Tami. I don't want to have anything to do with you. You already got me in trouble with Susan and Jughead is threatening to kill me if he sees me with you!" I should have just left but there wasn't enough room for me to drive the car past her vehicle.

"You still mad that I told Stanley about us? He won't do anything as long as I stay quiet – and happy. That's where you come in, keeping me happy." Tami licked her lips and clicked her tongue.

"Why me? You have all those men coming over to your party house. Why are you after me?" I was dumbfounded by her attention.

"Well, Roger-honey, I want to get out of here. I want to get as far from here as I can.

You don't know what it's like. I have to work in the party house every night, with men touching me all over. Pa sells me out to them and Jughead gets mad. If I don't do what they say, either one is likely to beat me.

"But you, you've been places. You've been in the world; you know how to get around. And the way you treat your wife, like she was some kind of friggin' princess! That's how I want you to treat me – I'll make you happier than you've ever thought possible." Tami bent over from the waist and wiped dirt off her left boot. She stood back up, smiling. "We all know you have money hidden away from your scam."

"What? I don't have any money. I wouldn't be living like this if I had money." I struggled but managed to shift my gaze directly to her eyes. All the warning signals in my brain were ringing but it was difficult to be unaffected by her.

"Pa said no one could cheat as many people out of their money as you did and not keep some of it for themselves. He says that you're playing dumb right now until the heat is off. You'll get your money later." Tami definitely overestimated my intelligence.

"Believe me, I don't have any money. Even if I did, I wouldn't go off with you. I love my wife. What do I have to do to convince you?" I leaned back against the Buick.

Tami came over, stuck her booted foot on the fender of the car, and rubbed her leg against me. "You better not worry about convincing me but worry about convincing your wife."

That's when I heard the sound of a vehicle arriving. I turned my head and there was Susan, pulling up in the truck to drive me home from work. I had not had a chance to tell her about the Buick.

Susan got out of the truck and slammed the door behind her. She walked straight up to Tami.

"You listen to me, you bitch. If I catch you around my husband again, I'll rip your ears off. Do you understand me?" Susan was fuming and at that moment, I thought she was going to rip her ears off right there, and then mine.

"Wait, Sugar. You got it all wrong..." Tami stopped in mid-sentence as Susan stuck her finger in her face.

"I don't have anything wrong. I know the type of girl you are. Leave us alone or I WILL hurt you." Susan's face was red and she kicked Tami's foot off the car. "Keep your legs to yourself."

"Sure, Sugar. You don't have to get mad." Tami turned on her heel, got in her truck, and left.

Susan turned back towards me. "If I had any other place to go, I would go there now. Get in the truck."

"Buddy gave me this Buick to drive for a while." I didn't want to make her any madder.

"Then get in the Buick and go home!" Susan muttered under her breath as she climbed back into our truck and drove off.

Chapter 14

Even though I had a job, our money was dwindling quickly. Susan tried to find work anywhere within a reasonable driving distance but she was always turned down. Between the pictures on the website and the stories of our conflicts with the Littles, no one wanted anything to do with us. After a couple of days, Susan finally spoke to me again, but I still had to sleep in the second bedroom.

On Friday night, I lay in my bed, sweating. The music from down the street was particularly loud and there was a lot of traffic on the road.

Over the music, several shots rang out, which wasn't unusual. The Littles often celebrated with gunfire and we were growing accustomed to it. Tonight though, something was different. After the gunshots, the music came to an abrupt halt and voices were shouting excitedly. Several cars came roaring by the house at high rates of speed and without their usual horn beeps of departure.

Then there was silence. I lay there another fifteen minutes but still no sound. I slowly dozed off.

Bam! Bam! Bam! Three hard bangs on our door jerked me wide-awake. I jumped to my feet, grabbed my nearby baseball bat, and ran to the door.

I swung the door open and there was Jughead. He was standing with his arms outstretched towards me. He was covered in blood, it dripped off his forearms and onto the front stoop.

"I done killed my brother." Jughead spoke to me with tears in his eyes.

I slammed the door and locked it.

"What was that about?" Susan walked up behind me.

"Jughead is outside, covered in blood, and said that he killed his brother. I'm going to call the State Patrol." I grabbed my cell phone and dialed the phone.

It took the patrolman about thirty minutes to get to our house. I first had to convince them that they needed to come rather than the Chattahoochee Valley Police.

The sharply dressed Patrolman took my statement on what happened and looked at the blood spots on the front steps.

"I'd like for you to come with me to help identify the man who came to your house." The Patrolman motioned towards his car and we rode down to the Little's shack.

The Little's yard was somewhat illuminated by a security light on a pole. We saw no one hanging about, which was unusual. The Patrolman turned on his blue lights and spoke through the car's loud speakers. "This is Patrolman Hicks of the Georgia State Patrol. Everyone, please come out to the front yard."

Out came the Littles. They came from the house, from the sheds, and from the miscellaneous cars sitting around. Many of the cars were just junk vehicles with no tires, missing hoods, and broken glass. However, even those cars were homes for someone, and sometimes they housed several residents.

As the people gathered round, Patrolman Hicks stepped back closer to the patrol car and I moved closer to him. There were at least fifty people around us chattering, asking what we were doing and what was going on.

"Settle down." The Patrolman yelled. "I'm here to check out a reported shooting."

"Who got shot, Officer?" It was Pa Little.

"I'm not sure but a 'Stanley Little' claims that he killed his brother." The Patrolman remained calm.

"Stanley's not here. I haven't seen him all day. Anybody seen Stanley today?" Pa Little looked around his group. They all shook their heads. A few emphatically said "No."

"Couldn't have been Stanley. He's not here. Besides, if anyone was shot, I'd know about it. We're all just trying to get some sleep." Pa Little smiled at the Patrolman.

"Mind if I look around?" The Patrolman was already walking towards the house. I was close behind.

"What are you doing here, Roger?" Pa Little asked as I walked by.

"He reported that Stanley Little came by his house covered in blood. I asked him to come with me." The Patrolman answered for me. Pa Little gave me a cold stare.

"Who's in the truck over there?" Pointing towards Pa Little's truck, Patrolman Hicks shined his flashlight into the cab. "Is that man alright?"

"Oh, don't mind him. He just had a little too much to drink and he's feeling a mite ill. He'll be alright tomorrow when he sleeps it off." Pa Little gave a flippant wave of his hand towards the truck.

"He's not going to drive like that is he?" Walking closer to the truck, Patrolman Hicks unsnapped his gun holster.

"Drive? Drive! No, he's not going to drive. Like I said, he just needs to sleep it off." Pa Little stepped between the officer and the truck. "You don't want to wake him. He can be a mean drunk when he's disturbed."

"Open the truck door." The Patrolman directed.

Reluctantly, Pa Little opened the truck door. The man fell out of the truck and onto the ground. Rolling the man over, the Patrolman aimed his light. Blood covered the front of the man's shirt from a gaping wound.

Around us, the Littles closed in on us. The Patrolman pulled his pistol and pointed it into the air. "Back up! I want all of you to back up!"

I was facing the crowd with my back towards the Patrolman, our escape blocked by the pickup truck. One of the Littles in front of me pulled a pistol from his belt. I instinctively tried to take another step backwards, tripped over the man lying on the ground, and then fell.

Someone from the crowd fired a gun. The bullet struck the State Patrolman in his leg. The Patrolman fired back, the shot found it's mark in his assailant's chest.

The crowd closed in on him rapidly. He fired two more rounds before they wrestled him to the ground and then proceeded to beat him with an assortment of fists, bats, and pipes.

Unarmed and already on the ground, I was no one's target at that particular moment. The Littles were all intent on the Patrolman. I rolled under the truck. In the scuffle, the Patrolman's gun dropped, I found it near me and grabbed it.

"Pa's been shot!" One of the Littles yelled out.

In the hushed silence that followed, the Littles moved back and formed a circle around the men. From beneath the truck, I saw three people lying on the ground – the man from inside the truck, Patrolman Hicks, and the third was Pa Little.

"Get him in the house! Go get Ma!" The Littles sprang into action. The commotion had everyone distracted so I rolled to the other side of the truck, slipped out, and made my way towards the edge of their yard.

I hid behind a shed and dared to chance a look back. They were carrying Pa Little into the house. Patch was helping direct everyone, "Where's that guy Roger? Find him!"

Several men in the crowd broke away and started the search for me. I turned to escape further into the woods but there was Yuri, on his unicycle even at this time of night. I expected him to start ringing his bicycle bell. Instead, he pointed to a small opening underneath the shed.

Not knowing the woods, and not being a great runner, I had few choices. I dove into the small opening but not all of me would fit. Yuri pressed his finger to his lips for me to be quiet and tossed a couple of bags full of trash on top of me.

Stifling my breathing as much as possible, I lay motionless, except for my excessively beating heart. My heart thumped so loud in my ears that I thought everyone heard it.

"Did you see a man run through here, Yuri?" I recognized Patch's voice. He was only four or five feet away. Now I would find out if this was just a trick on Yuri's part to trap me.

Yuri said nothing but Patch yelled out, "He pointed down towards the creek. Some of you circle 'round in case he tries to get to the road."

The footsteps ran off deeper into the woods, and the voices grew fainter. Yuri pulled the trash off me and pointed towards the police car.

I squeezed out from my hiding spot and shook Yuri's hand. The hand had an odd shape and I felt a couple of lumps in the palm.

Keeping a low profile, I ran to the patrol car. As most troopers tend to do, Patrolman Hicks had left the engine running. The Littles must have moved Hicks and the other man for they were nowhere to be seen.

Once in the car, I barely clicked the door closed and eased the cruiser into reverse. The blue lights were still flashing. Debating if I should leave them on or off, I left them on. I figured the sudden disappearance of the lights would draw immediate attention.

With my heart pounding and my hands shaking, I slowly backed out towards the driveway. The blue lights lit up the surrounding scenery in circles, presenting a glowing strobe light effect. I was close to the road, just a few more feet to go. I was almost out of the yard, still not free, but with a much better chance of living.

As I backed into the road, a car drove by and the driver honked his horn a couple of times. From the house, I heard someone yell out, "There he is! He's in the cop car!"

Discovered, I roared backwards into the road and slammed the cruiser into drive. I smelled burning rubber as the tires spun, trying to gain traction. Then the car launched forward. The powerful Police Interceptor engine roared down the quarter of a mile to our house.

Sliding into the driveway, Susan was standing at the front door, still in her house robe with her Angry Birds pajamas underneath.

"Get in the car! Get in the car!" I threw open the door and ran to her, pulling and pushing her along.

"What's going on? I heard the gunshots. Where's the State Patrolman?" Susan was hesitant but I kept urging her along.

"I'll tell you in the car on our way." I heard tires squealing down the road and two cars roared out of the Little's driveway. "We have to go now!"

Opening the passenger door, I forcefully pushed her into the car and ran to the driver's side. Susan screamed from inside the car, "Where? Where are we going?"

"I don't know." I threw the cruiser into gear but the Buick blocked my forward path. Behind me, one of the Littles cars pulled in crossways, blocking the driveway escape.

"Hold on." Reversing the car, I floored it. Driving backwards, we rammed into the rear-end of the Little's car. Both of our cars spun out into the highway.

One of the Littles lay in the road, thrown from their car on impact. Our car leaped forward and we sped down the road.

"Tell me what is happening and why you have that gun!" Susan hit her head when we rammed the car and her forehead was bleeding.

"It's the State Patrolman's pistol! They tried to shoot me and shot him instead. There was a fight and Pa Little was also shot. I barely got away but now they're chasing us." I forgot about having the pistol. "Patrolman Hicks was shot at least twice. I'm sure he's dead. Three people were down in all."

"What about Jughead? What happened to him?" Susan took the pistol and checked the ammo. "There's only two bullets left."

"We never saw Jughead. This all happened after we found a man shot in a pickup. I believe that was Jughead's brother." Glancing in the rearview mirror, the headlights of the Littles' cars were not far behind but we had a decent head start.

"Where are we going now?" Susan rummaged through the glove compartment and found a half box of ammo. She re-loaded the gun, put the remaining ammo in her pocket, and then buckled her seatbelt. "You better put yours on, too."

"We can't go to the Chattahoochee Valley Police and chance Deputy Justus being there. I doubt we can make it to the State Patrol station; it's at least thirty minutes away. I say we go to Turn On Inn. It's a public place and it's the closest place." I drove as rapidly as possible on the dark road, sometimes too fast. The tires squalled in complaint on the sudden sharp turns as we skidded across lanes.

"Don't you kill us before we get there!" Susan grabbed hold of the armrest to steady herself. "What was that?"

"I don't know! It's like it's out of gas but there's more than half a tank." The cruiser shuddered and briefly lost power. I felt no response from the accelerator pedal. It then caught up and shot forward again.

"The impact with the Littles' car must have damaged something." Back up to speed, the vehicle lost power again and the 'Check Engine' light came on. It then surged once more.

The Littles caught up to us. They drove the older style police surplus Crown Vics, both black, still with the push bars on front. One car rammed us from the back while the other tried to pass us. I barely cut him off.

They were side-by-side behind us, waiting for me to make a mistake. An approaching car flashed its lights, warning us that we were in their lane. I held my position and the Littles held theirs, blocking the path of the oncoming car.

Susan gasped and braced herself for impact. The approaching car finally ran off the road and into the ditch to avoid the head-on collision. Immediately, one of the Crown Vics pulled out to pass me on the left.

The cruiser shuddered again. "Hold on!" I yelled at Susan. With no power, I only had one defense. I slammed on my brakes.

The car that was passing roared past us. The car behind us crashed into the rear of our car. To my shock, instead of stopping or crashing, the rear car kept going – pushing us down the highway, gaining speed.

In front of us, the brake lights of the other car burned bright. Trapped between the two vehicles, with no power, we had nowhere to go.

Then the cruiser responded again. The engine roared to life once more. I jerked the wheel to the left and lurched into the other lane, barely clipping the tail light of the front car.

"They're attached to us!" Susan looked behind us. The rear-end collision had locked our cars together.

I tried to break us free. Swerving side to side, braking, accelerating, none of it worked. The cars clung together as if welded. The Littles continued pushing us down the highway.

Up ahead was an old church. I swerved to the right and into their big parking lot, hoping to free the cars with a sharp turn. Instead, the push car caused me to overshoot the driveway. We jumped their cement culvert, and skidded into the ditch. The impact broke the cars free.

Staying on the accelerator, Susan and I lurched back onto the road swerving wildly. The Little's car skidded off into the parking lot.

"Turn On Inn is only a mile away. If the cruiser holds up, we might make it." I glanced over at Susan. "You okay."

Susan's face was white. She nodded her head weakly. "Are we going to die?"

"No. We're going to get help. We're going to fight if we have to but we're not going to die. We're not letting these backwoods lunatics kill us." Glancing in the rearview mirror, I saw two sets of car lights still coming after us. In front of us was the sad glow of the Turn On Inn.

Chapter 15

———————

Sliding the cruiser into the parking lot of the Turn On Inn, we jumped out of the car, and ran to the front door.

"Hey! Hey! You can't park there! And turn those blue lights off." Security at the door blocked us from going inside. He pointed at Susan's attire. "And you can't wear pajamas in the bar except on Pajama Night!"

"Are Buddy and Hoss here? I have to see them now. It's an emergency!" I pleaded with the man. Reluctantly he let us in but stayed at the door to keep an eye on us.

Buddy, Hoss, and the band were just taking a break.

"Hey Roger! I didn't expect to see you here. What's up?" Buddy slapped me on the shoulder.

"It's the Littles. They shot a State Patrolman tonight and now they're after us. They will be here any second!" There was no time for me to explain everything.

"Go get Tiny. Tell him the Littles are coming." Hoss directed Security as he sprang into action. He removed his pistol from its holster and checked it quickly.

"You know how to use that? I was in the marines." Buddy motioned at the pistol in Susan's hand.

Susan looked down at the weapon and handed it to Buddy.

"Good." Hoss turned and spoke to the few bar patrons around the room. "Folks. Sorry to bother you but there may be some trouble here in a few minutes. It's the Littles. If you don't want to be part of it then I suggest you leave – immediately. If you stay, arm yourself with some sort of weapon."

Everyone left except for the four of us, two other members of the band, and Security.

"What's the trouble, Hoss?" Tiny, the owner, came out of the kitchen with a sawed off shotgun in his hand. He tossed a baseball bat to me. Security removed a blackjack from his hip pocket. The rest armed themselves with pool cues. "Did anyone pay their tabs before they left?"

"They're here." Security was watching out the window.

As I explained the situation, the front door burst open and in walked the Littles – six of them, with Jughead in front.

"I don't want no trouble in here." Tiny addressed the group.

"Just give us those two and there won't be any." Jughead waved his hand toward Susan and me. He took a step towards us.

"Stop right there." Hoss stepped in front of him, his pistol leveled at Jughead.

"Why all this hostility? Their car broke down and we just want to give them a ride home – being good neighbors." Jughead took another step.

"Last warning." Hoss pulled the hammer back on his gun and steadied his aim.

A deafening roar and flying shards of glass interrupted his shot. The windows behind us shattered as other members of the Littles clan ambushed us with shotguns. Bloody holes appeared across Hoss' body as buckshot ripped through his flesh. With the burn of at least one of the buckshot in my thigh, I went down and hit the floor hard.

The entire bar exploded with action. Both barrels of Tiny's shotgun blazed as he unleashed his weapon on the Littles. One of them went down. Another fell against the wall, but he wasn't out of the fight. He drew a pistol and shot Tiny three times.

Jughead was blasting away with his favorite gun, the Ruger LC-9. Buddy was in a firing stance. He shot one of the Littles and hit Jughead in the arm before Jughead landed a fatal shot to Buddy's head.

"I love this gun!" Jughead was unfazed by his injury.

Trying to shoot one of the band members, a Little came too close to me. I swung with the ball bat and hit him in the knee, hard enough to hear it crack. He went down and dropped his gun. I rose up, swung down, and cracked his skull with the bat.

Another Littles was reloading his shotgun. I hit him in the stomach with the bat but took a hard hit to the side of the head from Jughead.

My vision blurred, the room spun around, and the muffled sounds in the room fought with the roaring in my head. I felt I was going to be sick.

"Get the woman." Jughead's words slurred through my head.

"Roger! Roger!" Susan yelled at me.

I tried to get to my feet but Jughead kicked me again, sending me back down to the floor. He kicked me again in the face. I heard my nose crunch.

Two of the men approached Susan. When they grabbed her, she hit one of them square in the nose. The man hit her and her head snapped back.

Jughead was on him in an instant. He punched and kicked the man mercilessly. "Don't you hit her! Don't you ever hit her! She's mine!"

Jughead moved from the bloody man, looked at his other kinsmen, and glared at each of them. "Don't any of you touch her unless I tell you. She is mine."

The door to the bar opened and Deputy Justus walked in.

"You got a mess here, Jughead. We have three calls about a fight. And what is that wrecked patrol car doing out there?" The Deputy pointed towards the parking lot.

"There's a dead patrolman in my trunk. He goes with the patrol car. I'll need some help cleaning this up." Jughead looked around at the carnage.

"We have to get you out of here. It won't be long before someone calls the State Patrol and they will take all of you in for sure." Deputy Justus shook his head.

"Bring the cop's body inside and burn the place down – burn the cop car, too." Jughead grabbed Susan by the arm. When she resisted, he struck her hard and knocked her out. He half carried, half dragged her out the door.

The other Littles prepared the bar. Patrolman Hicks was dragged inside and his car doused in gasoline. They poured gasoline all over the inside and outside of the bar.

"What about him?" Someone nodded at me.

"He's not getting up. Leave him." Another replied.

"I'll stay behind and wait as long as I can before calling the fire station. That should give the bar plenty of time to get a good burn going." The Deputy took out a pack of matches.

Whoosh! A tossed match ignited the gasoline and flames licked the walls. The room quickly filled with smoke.

I coughed. The first real reflex I'd managed since knocked down. I coughed again and managed to get on my hands and knees. I painfully dragged myself forward.

My hand hit an object on the floor. It was the Patrolman's pistol. I instinctively latched onto the gun, for the second time that night.

The flames were getting higher. I stumbled to my feet and made my way to the broken window. Between the leaping and growing flames, I saw Deputy Justus standing next to his police car. He was on the radio with his back towards the burning building and me.

Despite the flames and glass, I crawled through the window and fell to the ground.

Justus finished his call and turned around. He spotted me and quickly reached for his gun. I shot him dead on the spot.

In the distance, approaching sirens wailed. I had to make a decision. Wait for the arrival of the police and hope they believe my story, as I stood there next to a dead cop whom I just shot with a dead patrolman's gun. My other option was to go get Susan myself.

I limped over to the Chattahoochee Valley police car and got inside. They were expecting Deputy Justus so this would be good cover.

I drove back down the road towards the Littles and flicked off the blue lights as I sped into the night.

Chapter 16

The ride back to the Littles seemed to take forever. I drove fast, though less recklessly than before. Blood running into my eye blurred my vision.

The only thing left in my life was Susan. No family, dead friends, deserted career, forgotten community. I had to get Susan back. All we had left was each other.

Stopping at our place, I drove the police car around to the back of the house. I checked the pistol. There were five cartridges left. With a few well-placed kicks, I finally freed the lock that secured the Deputy's shotgun to the dash. It held five shells. I noticed the Deputy's cell phone on the seat of the car and stuck it in my pocket.

Sticking the pistol into my belt and wiping the blood off my face, I set off down the path to the deer stand. Working my way through the brush was harder at night with no flashlight and the half-moon provided little help.

Finally finding the deer stand and following the trail, I eventually made my way down to the road. I was fifty yards below the Littles' house.

Two people were guarding their driveway. Taking a chance that they were more concerned with cars coming from the other direction, I quickly crossed the road, running in a low crouch.

The trail wound through the woods on the Littles' side of the road. Eventually, it ended at the edge of the Littles' back yard. All the lights were on inside the house except for the very back room.

There were cars in the back yard also. I crept slowly past them in case they contained any occupants. Finally, I made my way to the back of the house but still had no idea where to find Susan.

I heard muffled voices in the front yard – sometimes excited – sometimes commanding. Remembering the cell phone, I turned it on and used the camera to see around the corner of the house. Several people were rushing about and I definitely saw the two black Crown Vics. Susan had to be here.

Moving along the back wall of the house, I found the back door. It was unlocked and barely creaked as I eased it open.

The room was not completely silent. I heard the sounds of breathing and it was definitely from more than one person. I chanced the cell phone again and used the glow of the screen to glance around the room.

I was in some sort of nursery. Several cribs lined the walls and there was a rocking chair in one corner. The babies were sleeping.

Across the room was a closed door which I assumed lead to the main part of the house. Nearing the door, I glanced into one of the cribs and nearly dropped the cell phone. Inside the crib, the child must have been five years old. With a head shaped like Jughead's, it had a distended belly and legs too small to support its weight. It opened its eyes and chortled at me.

Quickly checking the other cribs, I found similar children. Disfigured, they ranged in age from newborn to several years old. I shook it off. This wasn't my concern.

At the door, I heard voices on the other side.

"Justus should have been here by now." Jughead's voice was easy to recognize.

"Anything could be holding him up. There will be fire trucks and law officers to be dealt with. It may be quite some time before he gets here." That was Patch's voice.

"Call him." Jughead bluntly commanded Patch.

Realizing that I had the Deputy's phone in my hand, I frantically searched for the volume buttons. The screen flashed on and read 'Patch' across the front. Already vibrating, I finally found the volume but it was too late. The phone played the theme from the Dukes of Hazzard.

"Hear that? That's Justus' ringtone coming from the nursery!" Patch threw open the door.

I barely stepped back out of the way. With the shotgun from the police car, I fired a load of buckshot into his chest. Patch fell backwards; the patch over his eye fell off and revealed a dark, crusty, pus riddled hole where his eye had once been.

As Jughead dove for his pistol on the coffee table, I ejected the spent shell from the pump shotgun and fired again. The blast blew a hole in the couch but missed Jughead.

Jughead landed on the coffee table, knocking cocaine and various other drugs all over the floor. He grabbed the gun and fired at me, holding me at bay behind the nursery door as he made his way towards an escape.

He leapt through the window and out into the yard. I chanced a shot out the window but was met with the Littles return fire.

A different door led from that room to Lil' Tami's Playhouse. Knocking open the door, I shot a man running straight at me. I had one shotgun shell left.

Susan was lying on the couch, bound and gagged. I made my way over to her and removed her gag, laying the shotgun down as I worked on the bindings on her hands.

"Roger! Behind you!" Susan screamed at me.

I rolled over and took a glancing blow to my back. I pulled the pistol from my belt and fired two rounds into my attacker. He fell to the floor.

Susan worked her way through her remaining bindings and freed herself.

"They were going to make me work in here, in the party room. Jughead said I was going to be his girl, and Tami's." Susan lolled her words slightly. "They gave me some kind of shot."

"We're going to get out. We'll have to go out the back way. Can you make it?" Grabbing the shotgun, I helped Susan to her feet.

"I think so. I just need to clear my head. You've been shot! And your head is bleeding!" Susan noticed my injuries. The shock seemed to wake her up some.

"Those are from earlier. I'll be okay. Let's try to move." I helped Susan towards the door to the next room.

"You better give up. You're not going to get out of there." Jughead yelled at us. A shot rang out and a bullet struck the jukebox causing a spray of sparks to fly across the floor.

Jughead and a kinsman charged through the door from the living area. I quickly fired two rounds but only struck the second man. Susan raised the shotgun but Jughead knocked it away. The shot went uselessly into the floor. He hit Susan hard in the face.

I rushed him but he hit me in the side of the head with his pistol. I lost my grip on my own gun and tried to fend off another blow with my forearm.

Jughead grabbed me by the neck and dragged me across the floor. Susan lay helplessly in a heap.

He hauled me out into the yard, in front of the lights from the cars, and knocked me to the ground. The rest of the Little clan gathered around.

"With Pa dead, you questioned me as the new leader. I may not be the eldest Little, but I have more children here than any other man. That gives me special rights. I'm going to show you that I can protect and lead the Littles as well as any." Jughead put the gun to my head as he spoke to the crowd of Littles.

"You're strong with a gun but they all know you can't beat me in a fight." From my hands and knees, I spat blood into the dirt.

"Can't beat you! I was giving you the easy way out. If you want to die slowly, that's your choice. Get him to his feet." Jughead laid his gun on the hood of a car.

I struggled to stand on my feet. If I bought enough time, maybe Susan would be able to get away.

Blood nearly blinded me in one eye and my leg was stiff from the buckshot. My head rang from the blows I'd already taken. I put up my fists.

Jughead came in hard, striking me in the head, cutting me with his sharp knuckles. I took the blows and blocked the brunt of the attack. Jughead took a wild swing. I blocked and landed a solid blow to his exposed ribs.

The blow knocked the wind out of Jughead. I took advantage of his brief surprise and landed two more solid body shots. Jughead covered his belly and I hit him with a roundhouse punch to the side of the head. Jughead went down.

Sensing victory, I stayed on top of Jughead, landing blows as fast as possible. I hit him repeatedly with lefts and rights and landed a thunderous roundhouse punch. I had him.

However, the other Littles would not allow that. Someone struck me from behind and knocked me off Jughead. He quickly recovered and kicked me in the face. I was now on the receiving end of his rampage. I don't how many blows and kicks he landed. I believe he finally just got tired of hitting me.

With an almost animalistic sound, he grabbed my leg and dragged me across the gravel driveway. The gravel cut into my skin. Stopping, he rammed my face and slammed my head into the gravel, creating fresh cuts. He kicked me with his steel-toed boots and I felt my ribs crack. Breathing became difficult and gasping for air was impossible.

"No! Stop! No more!" I'd had enough punishment but I did not have enough breath to shout. I was ready for the bullet to end it all. I could take no more.

"Go get the bolt cutters." Jughead commanded.

"You want to be a hero? You think you can go up against us? Try it with only nubs for fingers." Jughead held out the bolt cutters for me to see. "And your wife will be working for us! It won't take me long to get her to cooperate. She'll learn. Just like the rest of our girls."

Jughead put one of my fingers into the bolt cutter and clamped down. The pain shot up through my arm and shoulder. I grabbed my hand. My finger lay on the ground beneath me, still twitching.

He put my next finger into the bolt cutter.

An explosive single shot rang out. Jughead stopped in mid-action and fell forward on top of me. Turning, I saw Susan with the pistol. She had shot Jughead in the back of the head.

"Hoss said that you had to stand close with an LC-9. Guess it really wasn't your lucky gun." Susan still had the pistol aimed at Jughead.

The other Littles immediately turned on Susan. She pulled the trigger again but that was the last round. She stepped back towards the house, right into the dirty clutching hands of two of the Little men. She screamed as the hands seized her and dragged her to the ground. The others closed in on her.

In the distance and growing louder, wailing sirens pierced the night air. With blue lights flashing, several State Patrol cars pulled into the driveway. The first one barely missed running over me.

Patrol officers exited their cars with guns drawn. "Everyone! Step back and put your hands up!"

The Littles scattered like roaches exposed to the kitchen light. The ones that reached the woods disappeared into the night. Patrol officers chased after them but the Littles knew all the nooks and crannies where a person could hide.

It took the officers a while to establish order. The violent noises from before were replaced with the sounds of squawking radios and the patrol officers' orders. In the end, they managed to round up a few of the Little men.

I lay there in the rocks and dirt, aching in every part of my body. I tried to roll over onto my back.

"Stay still, mister. The ambulance will be here soon. Are you Roger Multry?" A patrolman knelt over me and gently pushed me back to the ground.

"Yes." I whispered the word but, even so, excruciating pain racked my ribs and back. "My wife?"

"She's okay. Here's the ambulance now, so try not to move. They'll take care of you." The patrolman waved his hand at one of the EMTs and yelled, "Over here!"

Vaguely conscious, I was aware of the flashing blue and red lights of the emergency vehicles. The EMTs stabilized me and laid me on the gurney. The lights swirled around and around in the trees and briefly highlighted the medical technicians' faces as they worked on my major injuries. They stopped the bleeding from my severed finger and removed several small pieces of gravel from my eye socket. The buckshot removal would have to wait for the hospital.

When they finished, the EMTs allowed Susan to join me in the bright lights behind the ambulance. Wrapped in an emergency blanket and still in her Angry Birds pajamas, both of Susan's eyes were black and her left cheek swollen. She took my five-digit hand. "You look a mess. Are you alright?"

"I think so." The IV, and the pain medication, made speaking a bit easier for me. "Remember the story of Chicken Little who thought the sky was falling? I think the whole damn sky just fell on top of me."

The patrol officers found the women of the Little clan hiding in the party bus in the yard. They ushered the women, young and old, out of the bus and gathered them around the lights of the ambulance.

Susan nudged me and pointed. Lil' Tami was there with the group in her cutoffs and boots.

"We will provide you ladies with medical assistance if needed." Near us, a patrolman spoke comfortingly to the group of women.

"Officer, are you going to arrest any of us women?" Ma Little stepped forward from the crowd.

"No, Ma'am. We don't have any warrants on the women." The officer smiled reassuringly at the ladies.

"Then we don't need your help. We have men folk to mourn." With that, Ma Little left the group and walked over to where Pa Little was being placed in a body bag.

"We know it's a sad day for you all. You've lost several of your loved ones." The officer watched as Ma Little bent over her husband's body.

"Officer, it's not a sad day. After all, there's a little Jughead inside all of us." Tami and several of the girls pulled up their shirts and rubbed their little poufy stomachs.

Chapter 17

The next day in the hospital, a representative from the United States Attorney's office visited Susan and me. He was dressed sharply in his custom suit, neatly pressed white shirt, and stylish shoes. The shoes looked like wingtips on top but had the soles of a comfortable walking shoe – very trendy.

"Hello, Mr. and Mrs. Multry. My name is James Randolph. I'm from the US Attorney's office, representative for Georgia. I have to tell you that we've been after the Littles for a long time. They have a history of crimes against the community – drug trafficking, child exploitation, human trafficking, prostitution, and now – murder.

"The problem we always have is getting witnesses to testify against them. They leave a trail of revenge and terror for anyone who speaks out. We lost two undercover agents, no trace, nothing to link their disappearances to the Littles. Now, thanks to you, we finally have the heart of the Littles." The attorney was excited, energetic, and very young. I recognized him after a while. His picture and name appeared frequently in the news – whenever there was a chance to advance his career.

"Are you saying you have all of the Littles?" Susan didn't sound like she believed him.

"Well, not all of them of course. They are a big family. We did arrest six people though. Four of them directly related to the recent events. We arrested the other two on outstanding warrants. We need your help to bring them to justice and break up their clan." If James Randolph was anything, he was earnest.

"Six people were arrested? That's all? There must be fifty or sixty of them, maybe more. What about the girls? What happens to them?" Susan was battered and bruised but her voice came through strong.

"You and your husband took care of the main people we were after – Pa, Stanley, and Patch – all dead. The girls? Nothing happens. They'll just go back to living the way they live." James Randolph glanced at his watch.

"The nursery?" Susan kept after him.

"Child Protective Services have taken the children from the nursery. Some of those children were eight and ten years old, still practically babies though." He shook his head sadly. "The other children will stay with the family."

"And Yuri? The boy with the football helmet. He helped me escape." I craned my neck around and looked at the man with my good right eye; the doctors told me that my left eye might never again be much use.

"We did spot a child wearing a football helmet several times, but we never got close to him. It was like trying to catch a wildcat. As we were driving away, he rode down the road beside us on a unicycle with that white helmet on his head. He was ringing a bicycle bell and making some rather obscene gestures at us. I cannot be certain what happened to him after that.

"We do have some other things to discuss." John cleared his throat, opened his leather briefcase, and pulled out a manila folder of documents.

"I'll get straight to it. We need your testimony. If you'll agree to serve as witnesses against the Littles, I have an official signed agreement that we can place you and your wife in the witness protection program." He showed us the first document.

"Before you agree, you have to know what you may be up against. The Littles have been known to seek revenge in the most violent of manners – and, as you pointed out, we don't have all the Littles.

"In addition, Pa Little had a brother – Lucas Little. He's a Southern Baptist revival preacher. We don't know exactly where he is or even if he knows that Pa is dead. Being a man of God, I doubt if he would come after you for revenge. However, in a case like this, you never know which is stronger – God or blood." He showed us a picture of a man a little younger than Pa Little, wearing a black suit and holding his Bible. "He hasn't been seen around here for years."

"What happens if we go into witness protection?" It hurt for me to speak even briefly.

"New names. New location. New job. They even agreed to drop the terms of your probation." He pulled out the final document outlining the witness protection program. "Do you have any special skills to use in your new identity."

I glanced over at Susan with my good eye. "Yes, as a matter of fact. Investment Broker!"

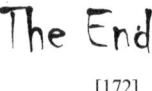

The End

About the Author

CJ Frye says that people have called him 'CJ' for so long that he no longer remembers what the initials represent. Enjoying relative privacy, CJ's novels are based on a category he calls "southern crimes."

Jughead is the first installment in CJ Frye's "southern crimes" series. Set in Palmetto and Rico Georgia, CJ Frye gives a local flavor to southern psycho terror.

On probation, banned from the only job he knows, out of money, Roger and Susan thought things couldn't get worse – until they are tormented by Jughead and his lawless, close-knit southern clan who wreak further havoc on their lives.

Publication is by Grace Garland Publishing. At Grace Garland Publishing, we are looking forward to CJ's next novel, which is awaiting publication.

Soon to be released
from CJ Frye

The Recruiter

In *The Recruiter*, CJ Frye continues his "southern crimes" series of books with a focus on Atlanta and the surrounding cities in the southeast.

When you look for a job, do you ever wonder what happens to all that information you supply? *The Recruiter* follows a staffing recruiter who is secretly wielding his own form of revenge on select job seekers.

Steven Banks lost his job, his wife, his future, and his thin grasp on reality. He blames the staffing conglomerate, GlobalNet, which is taking over American jobs and replacing them with well-trained, cheap foreign labor. Steven's answer: conduct serious candidate elimination.

Other Books from
Grace Garland Publishing

Chicken Nuggets

By Robert Tyson

Chicken Nuggets

by Robert Tyson

Robert Tyson presents a view into growing up in the sixties. Set in rural Carroll County, Georgia, his stories carry you back to humorous and strangely true events from his childhood. Run from a flock of terroristic chickens in Chicken Nuggets, take a momentary break in Outhouse Blues, look for an unknown creature in the dark of night in Red Eyes At Night, ride some unusual mounts in Horse Tales, or even learn the sport of Birding.

You'll enjoy a look back in time from his eyes!

Check us out at:

www.gracegarlandpublishing.com

and visit us on Facebook!

www.ingramcontent.com/pod-product-compliance
Lightning Source LLC
Chambersburg PA
CBHW071209260626
47162CB00004B/1230